985

the discovery of AMERICA

Excerpts from
the journal of
HARALD, the Younger

BRIAN CHERRY

QuickWorks

985 The Discovery of America

By Brian Cherry

Published by: QuickWorks
                 PO Box 463180
                 Mt. Clemens, MI 48046-3180

Distributed to the trade, specialty and consumer markets
by QW, Inc. (800) 838-8854

Editorial Director: Rebecca J. Ensign
Cover Design: Mark Sandell
Book Design: Michelle M. Ensign
Technical Support: Profit Makers, Ann Arbor, MI

Library of Congress Catalogue Card Number: 99-65792

10 9 8 7 6 5 4 3 2 1

160 Pages; Soft Cover; ISBN 1-928547-01-X; $14.95

Dedication

In memory of November 1, 1996

Acknowledgements

I would like to take this opportunity to thank the Cherry, Evo, Tocco and Romesburg families for their continued loving encouragement in just about everything I do.

Special thanks to my father and mother for putting up with me and Larry and Vicki Evo for keeping me well fed.

I extend my appreciation to Joseph Latta and Jon Angell of Black Sword Armory, Inc., makers of the finest weapons in the realm.

And, finally, I give my thanks to the Knights of the Trinity for all their help.

Foreword

In the year 985, a storm driven vessel sailed out of a fog bank and into clear view of the Canadian Coast line. This was the first recorded sighting of the continent of North America. Archaeological evidence conflicts on just who is to be credited with this first sighting, but one thing is clear—it was not an Italian with a poor sense of direction.

The first, and more than likely, incorrect, theory of discovery attributes the voyage to the adventurer and prince, Leif Eiriksson. This claim is supported by the often quoted and historically inaccurate "Eirik the Redds Saga." This literary work is the written history of the family of Eirik (archaeological sources place it as written no later than the year 1022) and is notorious for crediting members of the royal family with historically significant acts.

The second, and more believable scenario, gives credit to Bjarni Herjolfsson. Bjarni was a sailor whose ship was blown south of his intended destination of Greenland. A thick fog had settled in and due to his lack of visibility, he passed Greenland and continued west. When at last the fog had lifted, he was in view of North America.

Like today, events of great importance were recorded by historians, poets, journalists and scribes. This event was no different. The discovery of a new land was big news and though many of the accounts conflict in details, the event as a whole is well documented:

The Groenlendinga Sage of 1000
Eirik the Redds Saga of 1022
The Iclandic Annals of 1121 and 1347
The writings of Adam of Bremmen of 1075
The Journal of Harald the younger, 985-1066

While scholars still debate over the translations, and much of the original text will forever remain in its original form, the Journal of Harald the younger, discovered just over 200 years ago, is the most plausible account of Herjolffson's first voyage to North America and the ill-fated, subsequent colonization effort in the early 11ᵗʰ century.

While this author has made every attempt to preserve the original work's linguistic and historical accuracy, from time to time it became necessary to apply poetic license and inject speculative interpretation. As mentioned above, some passages in the original text are of such complexity, that they may never be able to be completely translated. Thus, only excerpts from Harald's journal, presented chronologically, can be published at this time. In addition, in the interest of providing the reader with a good story at an information age pace, contemporary language was often used in place of the labyrinthine language and syntax resulting from the initial scholastic translations. The result is a really good story.

985

the discovery
of AMERICA

Excerpts from
the journal of
HARALD, the Younger

Chapter 1

My name is Harald, Harald the younger, and I am seasick. One look at my shoes and a good bit of the deck around my feet, and anyone can see that I am not just seasick, I am very seasick. The inability to hold down my breakfast is unpleasant enough, but the fact that I am a sailor on this vessel makes the humiliation nearly unbearable. For the past hour, each time I looked at one of the hairy oafs on this ship, he would stick his finger down his throat, point at me and laugh until his bladder burst. The thought of some of the new names I'll get from these barbarians, like "Harald the Messy" or "Look out below Harald," makes Harald the younger seem very comfortable.

For most of my twelve years on Earth I have craved a better name. All my brothers have names inspired by kings, honored relatives and great deeds. Yet, I have been bestowed with a stupid name because I had the misfortune of being son number 13. After twelve sons before me, my parents simply ran out of kings, honored relatives and great deeds. I desire one of those names because those are names that men fear and for which women ovulate. Had I only been named, "Thorkell the Great" or "Eirik Bloodax." Although, those names weren't given at birth, they were earned. And to be fair, there were many a king bestowed with the name of Harald, as had countless other men and their thralls. I believe the term used to aptly describe my name is "common."

And so, in the tradition of journals written at sea, I make my first confession. I am on this ship to earn a name for myself. I need future generations to remember me for something more than being the last of thirteen sons. That position says more about the fertility

1

and stamina of my mother and father than it does about me. Right now, all history can say about me is that I was a stow-away sailor with a weak stomach and an aversion to herring.

Bjarni Herjolfsson, the captain of this ship, is my father's best friend. He was visiting for supper a few nights ago and I asked him if I could go on the voyage to Greenland with him. "My ship is no place for a twelve year old boy," he said, "We are bound for the colonies in Greenland and it may be years before we see Iceland again. I've no time to wet nurse you and tuck you in when you start to miss your mum."

With this said, I knew exactly how he felt about the value of adolescent boys. His stance on adolescent girls, however, was something altogether different and possibly the reason he was so eager to leave Iceland. That is a story for another day's telling though. The fact still remained that he was not going to let me on his ship.

Three days ago, I decided to be a stow-away. I scribed a note for my family. I told them not to worry and that I would return someday. I left my father a separate little note apologizing for any strain this decision would put on his friendship with Bjarni. I had no doubt that my father would understand why I was doing this. He was a firm believer in the adventures of youth. He often acted as a buffer between my mother and I. Mum had decided I was to be an educated man. I spent hours learning, not only my own language and history, but also Latin and the speech of the Anglos. My future as an intellectual was, as far as she was concerned, set in stone. She would brook no interference with this goal. She eventually wanted to see me become an ambassador or member of court.

This was not my goal. I wanted to live and acquire the possessions of great adventurers. I remember all the times my father would cover for me. He would pretend I was in my room at night and tell my mother I had gone to bed early. He would leave clean clothes behind the house so that I could change before my mother questioned the mess of my clothing that my evening's activities had made. It is amazing how dirty one can get while hiding in the bushes, watching Gretchen, daughter of Snorri the Thick, bathing. This time, my father cannot cover for me and I do fear my present decision will disappoint my mum.

Anyway, once I finished being "the good son," and left my parents an explanation, I snuck out to the docks. As I crouched between two herring barrels, I looked Bjarni's ship over. She was called "Mist." Her hull was wider and deeper than the conventional ships of our people. There was also a large cabin in the middle that served as Bjarni's home away from home. It maintained the Norwegian ships' basic shape and displayed the dragon's head and tail, but had been modified to sacrifice function for comfort.

I had once toured her with my father. I knew she had a large cargo hold below deck and a galley for the preparation of meals. It was obvious Mist was constructed for the sole purpose of allowing Bjarni to sail while enjoying all the comforts of his family's rather pampered lifestyle.

I concocted several plans to get on to the Mist. One by one, I ruled each out. The catapult, the complex tunnel system, the distraction fire using Scotsmen as decoys, were all good plans but required time that I didn't have. Just as I was about to give up, I began studying the barrels I had wedged myself between. They were marked for the Mist. Eventually they would wind up in the Mist's larder. So I jumped in one of them.

It was filled with salted herring. The slime from the fish soaked me to the skin. It was not a good kind of wet. It was the thick and heady wet of a newborn calf.

That was not the worst part. If I were not already twisted into the barrel, the stench would have doubled me over. Despite the horrible discomfort of my situation, the plan worked. I was simply carried on the ship with the rest of the supplies. Well, it really wasn't that simple.

I lived in the barrel for forty-eight hours. I would like to say that it was by design, but the truth of the matter is the motion of the boat had made me queasy and I fainted into a coma for eighteen of those hours. I was forced into regaining consciousness when two sailors, looking for dinner, opened the barrel. They reported my discovery back to Bjarni. He was silent when he entered the storeroom. It was hard to predict his degree of anger, for he was amazingly calm as he picked up his hammer, placed the lid on the barrel and nailed it shut. That is how I spent the next thirty hours.

It didn't take long for the rocking motion of the boat, combined with the cramped isolation and overwhelming smell of dead herring, to start working on my mind. When they finally got around to freeing me from the barrel, I was in the midst of some rather profound visions. For the most part, they seemed to be centered around an image of naked English women frolicking in porridge and hand feeding me bits of liver. Seeing as most of my dreams involve naked women feeding me, I thoroughly understood that part of the vision, but I was most unsettled about the porridge and liver, the two things I hated most in the world. (Until I was a guest in the herring barrel).

My burly colleagues dragged me to Bjarni's cabin and dropped me on the floor. By that time my legs were as limp as the herring.

"BOY," he bellowed in a voice that suggested he would make a superb thundercloud. "I DON'T LIKE STOWAWAYS! Every mouthful of food you eat is one less mouthful of food for my sailors. You're nothing more than ballast, and this journey is too risky for me to spend one second worrying about human ballast............" He said some other things but the naked English women came back and they were most distracting. "...............throw you over the side if it weren't for your father. What kind of friend would I be if his youngest brat got killed on my ship? So, since I can't kill you, and I can't feed you while you play sailor games all day, you're going to have to work for your passage. From now until we dock in Greenland, you are the thrall for the entire crew. Every menial, dirty, disgusting task aboard this ship is now yours. Your first duty will be to go down to the galley and start preparing fish for the cook..."

He said something about the fish, but I wasn't quite sure what it was. The English women came back and this time they were tossing balls of snow around his cabin.

"......and that reminds me of one more detail. We have no cabin or bunk for you so you'll be sleeping down in the hold with the supplies."

4

I smiled. (I saw one of the English women pouring porridge on Bjarni's head.) My smile seemed to pacify Bjarni. He pointed to my "quarters" and, with a twitch of his eye, instructed me to go there immediately...

Ah, yesterday, with its phantoms and visions, was truly a happy day. Now twenty-four hours later, my present moments are filled with a bad stomach, filthy shoes, and a sentence of indentured servitude to the entire crew. Worst of all, I am receiving no visits from the English women as I lay down to sleep.

About midday today, I started the noble task of potato peeling. To accomplish this mission, I was given a rusty spoon. It seems that part of my punishment is to be denied the proper tools with which to complete my assigned tasks. Cook gets a great laugh from this added torture.

Until I came to the Mist, I had never met anyone quite like Cook. He is far and away the ugliest creature I have ever met. He is hairless, with the exception of the thin spray of white behind his ears. His toothless grin and single eye make him difficult to look at during conversations. He is also shaped in the most peculiar fashion. If I squint a little, it is very difficult to tell the difference between Cook and the potatoes I have been peeling. He is also the closest thing I have to a friend on this ship. As I performed my galley duties, I heard many tales of Cook's glory years in the Norwegian navy.

"I tell you, lad, those were the good old days. Back then a colonization voyage meant sailing to another country and sticking it to the poor bastards, but good."

When Cook said the word "sticking," he drove his knife into the cutting board and began to laugh hysterically. I now know exactly what "colonization" means to Cook.

5

It was on our third day of the voyage that it happened. Cook was acting out another story. He was jumping about the hold cutting and jabbing at imaginary foes as his tale went on. He had reached a point in the telling where the required action was a pelvic thrust, when a strong wind hit the ship and sent Cook thrashing into the bulkhead. The gust hit with the force of a battering ram. My first thought was that a rogue whale had run into the ship. I rushed up onto the deck and watched the furious activity. I lacked the instinct to be of any immediate help.

"Tie down all loose objects, you twit! And if we don't need it, throw it overboard!"

It was difficult to hear his instructions, but I knew he was yelling at me. The sound of the water and wind punishing the ship added to my fear. A sailor ran toward the mast and began tearing the sails down. I began to scurry about tying down barrels of food, water and whale oil. When that was finished, I secured the hatches and took refuge in the hold.

Down in the storage area, the barrels were rolling free and spilling their contents all over the floor. I had assumed Cook stayed down below to secure the supplies, but upon my return I found the galley was a complete mess and Cook was nowhere to be found. I spent the next three hours securing fish barrels. I probably could have done this in less than an hour but I had an added challenge. The floor was coated with fish oil, my sea legs were only three days old, and the deck changed angles every other second.

After what seemed an eternity, I staggered to the corner of the hold and found the pile of blankets that I call my bed, and fell into them. I covered myself, turned on my right side and was suddenly looking into Cook's ear.

I sat up and pulled his covers back from him. At first I thought he was dead, but then he groaned. He wasn't dead, he just smelled that way. At his side lay four bottles of mead. I guess he thought the first step to securing the supplies was to make sure the liquor was safe. I remembered my earlier instructions to throw anything useless overboard. Cook qualified. I thought about this for a moment and decided that dragging him topside was far more of an effort then I was willing to put forth. So, I rolled him over, onto a small pile of twisted ropes, and went back to my blankets.

As I awoke, I noticed that the sailing was smooth and I thought I was finally going to experience some of the good thrills of being a sailor. I splashed my face with water and started up the ladder. About half way up, I heard Cook, presumably tangled in the ropes, cursing. I might have gone back down and unrolled him, but I was far too anxious to smell the sea air, and feel the breeze kiss my face as I watched the land come closer and closer to us…As soon as I got on deck my mood changed.

It was as if we had sailed straight up into the heavens…the fog was that thick. No sun, no stars, no horizon, just a few faces of those who were standing within four inches of me…that's all I could see. Even I could have navigated the ship at that moment, for doing so had been completely reduced to guesswork.

"All right, lads," Bjarni said, "It is business as usual." His voice seemed to be coming from where the prow of the ship had always been. He sounded steady and almost reassuring.

"Cook, are you there?"

"Aye, Captain, at your service," Cook said from below. I imagined he was only half untangled and fully hung over.

"We will need to start rationing our supplies immediately. We shall continue to sail in our present direction until we have passed through the fog bank. At that time, we will take fresh bearings and continue on to Greenland. All non-essential personnel will stand down and be confined to a state of rest until the period of rationing is over."

Then, Bjarni walked back to his quarters and I retreated to my blankets. At least the fog prevented anyone from seeing the look of panic on my face as I rushed to follow Bjarni's orders and rest. It seemed everyone knew how to go about their business in this situation. This is obviously nothing new to any of them. But as a first time, nonessential sailor, I feel lost and worried.

7

For the past several days I had been in the hold listening to Cook tell his tales. Just as he began telling another story that required the pelvic thrust, we heard the call of "LAND HO!" I rushed up the ladder and ran to the side where all the other men were standing and staring. I looked through what was left of the fog bank, out over the land. It was well forested with low hills, not at all what I had expected. I have heard that Greenland is a rocky, mountainous land. As I peered out at this land, I wondered how the colonists farmed with so many trees about. I also wondered why Bjarni was scowling and shaking his head.

"Captain Bjarni, sir," I said respectfully, "how soon before we dock?"

"I have no idea, boy."

He didn't look at me, but I'm sure he felt my bewilderment. It was that or he just had an affinity for dramatic pauses. Either way, he felt the need to elaborate upon his answer.

"That's not Greenland, I have no idea where we are." That was the last thing he said. And that was the last thing I wanted to hear.

Chapter 2

"We're doing what?" Exclaimed Sigtrig. "That bastard's not taking us home?"

His bellow shook the lower crew's quarters. Vocally disturbing the walls, regardless of its effect, was just not satisfying enough to Sigtrig. He went on to assault the walls with his fist, foot, shoulder, head, and the poor sailor who, momentarily putting aside his sense of self-preservation, was stupid enough to tell him of our new course headings.

Sigtrig the Bone Breaker was a big man. Well, actually he was a good bit bigger than big. He tended to be on the frightening side of mountainous. In a pinch, he could pass for a lunar eclipse. His name, the Bone Breaker, is one that was to be taken quite literally. He had been so named for the way in which he would dispatch an enemy in battle. He made the deliberate point of wounding them, and going on to snap as many bones as time allowed. This would eventually end with the neck, or in a fit of extreme cruelty, the spine. He would leave them crippled but not dead. In his view, thus denying them a trip to Valhalla. In short, he was not the correct man with whom to share bad news.

Making a point to heed my god given sense of self-preservation, I left the room just as his tantrum was beginning. I made my way up to the deck and watched the new land pass as we sailed along its shore. This was the decision that had brought Sigtrig to such a state of rage. We were following the shoreline instead of changing course to Greenland.

Bjarni saw the new land as an opportunity. The fact that it is here is really no surprise to anyone. It is said that if you climb a high

9

enough hill in Greenland and look west, you can see this land. Bjarni figured that it was just about time that someone actually took a look at it. With that notion firmly in his head, he turned the boat south to explore the coast. The problem is that Greenland is north. This decision didn't really sit well with a number of the sailors. Many of them were going there as colonists and were eager to check out their new home. Me, I don't really care. My home is in Iceland.

I watched the land for a little while. It didn't appear to be inhabited, but occasionally I could swear that I saw a face pop out of the brush. Of course if you stare at the moon long enough you can make out a face, and if you sniff dead herring for any extended period of time, Odinn only knows the things you're going to see.

The land itself didn't really seem to have much in the way of a beach. The tree line ended and water just picked up from there. It also seemed to be dominated by an endless series of low rolling hills. The forest went back for as far as the eye could see. I have never seen such endless greenery. I watched for what seemed like quite a long time. It was one of those quiet, contemplative moments the old ones are always going on so much about. Personally I'm bored stiff. I pushed myself away from the ledge and headed back down to my cot in the hold. I wonder how much dead herring we have on hand.

The last three days have passed slowly. Bjarni is still following the coast of the new land. For the most part, he is the only one who is enthused about this new find. The land itself is rather unremarkable and, in his own words, "good for nothing," but the prospect of going down in history as a discoverer has him excited to the point of irrational behavior. A day and a half ago provisions started running dangerously low. We all thought this would be our ticket to Greenland. No food means we have to turn back, right? Wrong, Bjarni took us all off our regular duties and had us fishing from sunrise to sunset.

This, plus the rationing of food and water, has morale very low. Part of rationing is restricting duties to essential ones only. A man who sits in bed all day doesn't have to eat as much. Of course, this leads to almost unbearable boredom. With the reserves of herring running low my recreational outlets were becoming numbered. I tried some of the fish we had caught yesterday, but the effect just was not the same. Usually an alternate cure for boredom was Cook and his inane stories, but as of late his subject matter had taken an uncomfortable turn.

Instead of his usual dottering on about his life with the navy, he was talking about what to do with our current problem. The word mutiny was being whispered between him and many of the crew. Their hushed tones could not hide their intent and that particular word made my toes itch and I wanted nothing to do with it.

It was about four in the afternoon when Bjarni gathered the crew on deck. He selected six men and prepared a landing boat. We stocked it and sent him on his way. He had gone to physically explore the new land. About an hour later, the boat returned with Bjarni trussed and barely conscious. We stared at him with his half open eyes and watched as he blew little spit bubbles. Eirik Hakonsson stepped out of the boat and began to explain what happened.

"We were rowing to the shore. Bjarni was telling us how famous we would be once we come back with this discovery." Eirik wrung his hand in an uncomfortable sort of way as he spoke. "He spoke of women and how they just spread for explorers."

Even in his partially conscious state, Bjarni started to drool at this point in the story. Eirik looked over at him, he was ringing his hands pretty hard at this point. He looked back at us and continued.

"We were almost there when Bjarni walked to the prow of the boat and yelled, 'on to Bjarni land.' He then removed a horn from his bag and started blowing it as we rowed. The rest is kind of blur to me, but what else were we supposed to do?"

He elaborated no farther. Bjarni lying on the floor of the landing boat, trussed and dazed with a big bump on his head and a broken oar next to him, told us the rest of the story. I wonder if he even got a note out of that horn before somebody took an oar across his face. Sigtrig carried Bjarni to his cabin tucked under one arm the way

11

someone would carry a sack of potatoes. He also sported a larger, more menacing smile than usual. It is more than likely that he was the captain's assailant. We got together after that and decided on a united story of a captain gone mad. It is after all, for the most part, true. We then turned the ship north and headed for Greenland.

Chapter 3

After about seven hours of being tied to his bed, unconscious, Bjarni regained consciousness. The yelling and screaming started almost immediately afterward. The din he made was absolutely atrocious. He screamed, cursed and on occasion, begged Odinn to smite us and our next ten generations. We had originally hoped that he would just scream himself out and be done with it. That was, however, not to be. We had learned, much to our chagrin, that his ability to be obnoxious was at a superhuman level. He had managed to maintain his verbal assault on the crew for nearly nine hours with no sign of any immediate let up. At times he would rattle off at least ten minutes worth of obscenities without any indication that he had even taken a breath. Had I not been going out of my mind with annoyance, I probably would have been extremely impressed.

A crewman by the name of Svain was assigned the glorious task of guarding the door of our beloved leader. He was there for the full nine hours of the tantrum. The longer Bjarni yelled, the more vacant the sailor's expression became. After a while, the combination of sun, hunger and Bjarni's grating voice seemed to be getting to Svain. His eyes glazed over. It was as if he were staring through everything on the ship and at something a thousand leagues in the distance. I watched him for a little while.

Svain was a longtime crewman of Mist. For the most part, he kept to himself and avoided personal contact with others. He was thin from the rationing of food and had been standing there all day listening to the racket. After a long time, something within him snapped and he did the unexpected. He drew his sword, knocked on Bjarni's cabin door, and went in. I don't know if it was too much

13

time in the sun or hunger from the rationing, or if he was just cocked that we weren't in Greenland yet. Either way it appeared that Svain made a decision that would leave our captain very dead.

Sigtrigg watched Svain go into Bjarni's cabin. Apparently, he noticed the drawn sword, the vacant eyes, and recognized Svain's intent. It wasn't a second and a half before he was running in there himself as if he were going in there to show him how to kill Bjarni properly. Heaven forbid there be a bloodletting without Sigtrigg participating.

The rest of crew just watched as the door slammed behind him. Most of us have expressed mixed feelings about our captain. He has, after all, taken us way out of our way and nobody is happy about the rationing. I couldn't speak for the rest at that moment, but I did not want to see him dead. Unfortunately, there was not a thing I could do about it. Most of us stared at the cabin door. It had been very quiet in there since Sigtrigg stormed in. Suddenly there was a crash. My body froze for a moment from the shock of the sound, but it felt as though my skin had leapt from my body to find a decent place to hide. Judging from the suddenly pale expressions around me, I wasn't the only one who had almost separated from his skin.

"Oops, sorry about that," Cook said.

He let go of a little chuckle as he picked up the bunch of metal plates that he had dropped. I guess he felt the tension in the air and couldn't pass up the chance to take ten years off each of our lives. There are times when Cook can be a real pisser.

I was still looking in Cook's direction when I heard a loud wet thud come from the Captain's Quarters. I almost dislocated my neck as I snapped my head toward the sound. It was embarrassing. After what Cook had pulled, I should have been more prepared for sudden noises. That thud was followed by another one just like it, then I heard glass breaking, metal clanking against metal, laughter, and then a scream. The door splintered as a body came through it. The crew surrounded what was left of what appeared to be our captain. I tried to force my way to the body but eventually, I settled for just getting on my hands and knees and trying to work my way through everyone's legs. I looked at the face of what was now a very dead sailor. It was not the face that I had expected to see. This was the man who had originally gone in, with sword in hand, to presumably kill Bjarni.

I looked in the direction of where the door used to be. The space was now filled by the massive frame of Sigtrigg. He had to turn a little sideways to go through the opening. End to end, his shoulders were wider then the door frame.

"He was going to kill the captain," Sigtrigg said.

Nobody dared ask him any questions. The dead man on the ground had his head twisted in a complete circle. His neck looked like a cloth with the water rung out. We were all too terrified to even look at Sigtrigg, let alone question his actions. The pause was very long. There was an extremely uncomfortable awkwardness about it. Obviously Sigtrigg felt this also. He took it upon himself to further explain this incident.

"Mutiny is one thing. Especially when your captain has gone sick in the mind, but killing him while he is helpless is something completely different. He is one of us, a Norseman, an Icelander. His god is Odinn, as is mine. To kill him while he is strapped to his bed would deprive him an honorable death in battle and damn him forever to Niffelheim. Odinn would curse us for such a deed and surely destroy this ship. None of us would make it home alive. At least Svain died in battle and is now with the gods as a hero."

With that, he wiped his bloody hands on his pants and disappeared into the crew's cabins. We crafted a small wooden raft from the wood of empty barrels. We put Svain's body on it, covered him with oil and sent him floating out to sea. Sigtrigg shot flaming arrows at the raft until it caught fire. Svain was put to rest in honorable fashion. To prevent any other crewmen from going crazy, it was decided that the ship's supply of mead would be transferred to Bjarni's cabin for the duration of the trip. We assigned someone to pour a pint down his throat once an hour. This kept him quite drunk, but at least he was quiet.

It seemed to be a nearly endless journey from our newly discovered land, but we have finally made it to Greenland. Our arrival didn't come a day too soon. The stocks of mead started to run low. Greenland looked just the way I had expected it to look. It was mountainous and rocky. I could see some fertile land close to the shore, but this was the illusion for which the land was named. To the naked eye it appears to be fertile, but once you get inland, you realize what a quarry the place really is. As we sailed along the shore line, I could see colonists working the land. They looked happy enough. Perhaps this may be a good place to settle for a while.

Once we had docked the boat, everyone quickly went his separate way. Leaving fast was a must in this case. To most, mutiny is a hanging offense. Traditionally, law enforcement in new colonies is a bit soft, but no one was willing to stay around long enough to test this theory. Each sailor on board had either someone waiting for him or somewhere to go. Even Bjarni had family living in Greenland. I would love to see the look on his father's face when he sees the state in which his son has been left.

I made several unsuccessful attempts to secure lodging. Cook refused to help me. He claimed that he was too old and lacked the strength to look after a young boy. It wasn't very long before I was the last one left.

"That's fine," I thought. "I don't need them. I got this far on my own. I'll simply fend for myself."

Lodging was simple enough. I have stowed away back on the boat. As long as it is docked, someone may as well use it for something. I thought it would probably be a while before Bjarni was able to come back to the ship. For now I can also live off what's left in the ship's larder. In the morning, I can set some rabbit traps and then look for work. Everything's going to be just fine. I know it.

It has now been three days and I'm just about out of food. Nobody seems to want a hired hand, at least not an inexperienced one. At this point I would trade my soul and any other substantial part of my anatomy for a rabbit. This day started out as the three previous days. I left the ship to check my traps. I set about eight or ten of them in the forest a mile or so away. I kept them well away from any populated area to increase my chances of catching something. It took me a couple of hours to check them all. At each one, it was the same story. The trap was sprung, but there was no rabbit. I have begun to think either this island is the home of some new breed of hyper-intelligent rabbits or I just stink as a trap maker. Considering the overall simplicity of a rabbit trap and my general mistrust of anything with big loving eyes and soft huggable fur, I am leaning to the former as a solution. Perhaps the world is fortunate that these genius bunnies have not yet discovered the secret of ocean travel. If they get off the island we may cease to be the world's dominant life form.

I find it necessary to shake my head several times to clear this thought from it. For, whenever I start worrying that rodents will take over the world, I am convinced that it's way past my mealtime. I just gave my head another good couple of shakes to be sure that the thought has truly gone.

After clearing my mind, I reset the traps. As I headed back to the ship, I reasoned that I had another couple day's staples and if I rationed carefully, surely by then I would have figured out what to do.

As I drew nearer to the ship, I could see activity on its deck. There were a good number of people on the ship and it appeared they were having a party. Bjarni's ship was adorned with many lights and decorations. As I began to make my way to the ship, the music stopped. I dove into a grove of bushes for fear that I had been spotted. I made some space between the leaves and branches of the bush so I could see what was going on. The partygoers were raising glasses in unison. I could hear someone speaking but could not make out what he was saying. It was obvious they were toasting something. They lowered their glasses and then there was a moment of silence. After that the music started. Bjarni's party was a rather good one by the looks of it. There was music, dancing, food, drink, nakedness, and there was the type of activity that my mother warned me would give me liver spots if I did it too young. I sat down behind my bush. For a change, Odinn seemed to be smiling on me. All I had to do was sit there, wait for the party to end and collect the leftovers. I could sleep when they all left the boat.

The music stopped. The men all raised their glasses to the air and then another moment of silence. I was beginning to wonder what that was all about until I looked up to where they were pointing. The yardarms of the ship were full of bodies hanging by the neck. They swayed in the breeze and looked like some macabre wind chime. I could not see the faces of the dead, but the silhouette of a huge man amongst those hung told me all I needed to know. That was Sigtrigg, the rest were Mist's crew. I wiped away tears as I thought of Cook and his last terrible last moments.

My first instinct was to run back to the forest and dive into a ditch. "I can't take anymore," I yelled. I have no food, no shelter, not even a blanket. I dove headlong into a deep hole near my third trap and remembered how my father always told me not to cry. It was easy not to cry when I was home. How I wished I were home. It was cold in the ditch. I wanted to be with my mother. I could no longer stop the tears. I pleaded with Odinn, "please get me out of this cold, wet, horrible place, please." I fell into a fitful sleep as I prayed.

I woke to what sounded like one of my traps springing. It took a few minutes for my eyes to adjust to the nighttime darkness. I stood up. My ditch was a little deeper than I thought. The opening was about a foot out of my reach. I piled some large stones together and used them as a footstool. I reached for the opening and pulled myself up and out. Once out of the hole I looked toward my trap. To my surprise, a half dozen pair of eyes were staring back at me. For starters, these eyes were not the loving eyes of the hyper-intelligent rabbits I so mistrust. These eyes were the malevolent, forward set eyes of a predator. The pupils almost glowed as they reflected the moonlight back at me. As my eyes adjusted to the dark, I saw pieces of what used to be a rabbit on the ground.

"One mystery solved." I thought to myself.

I didn't dare turn around because I knew there were more behind me. I had watched wolves hunt before. And, despite the fact that they are not supposed to be in Greenland, there they were. They began to move in on me and I knew that I was going to die.

I fell on my face and began to beg and cry as the wolves slowly came closer. I lifted my face out of the dirt just in time to see one of them lunge toward me. I closed my eyes and prayed that my death would be a quick one. I heard it snarl just before it landed. Then there was the sound of a high pitched scream and the unmistakable thud of an impact. To my surprise, the thud had nothing to do with the wolf hitting me. In fact, the wolf had never made it to me.

I opened my eyes and watched the animal run away. He had a long red streak of blood across his back and was howling in pain. One was down but how many more were there to go? I could only assume that the gods had taken pity on me and had come to my defense. Fire came from the sky and knocked another one of those wretched dogs back into the darkness. Behind me, I heard the horrific sound of the smiting of yet another wolf. It was at this point, I felt completely safe and secure so I allowed myself to pass out.

I awoke in a bed with furs blanketed on top of me. My first assumption was that the gods had taken me to Valhalla to nurse me back to health. This illusion was soon destroyed by the sight of a very non-godlike looking man coming to my bed with a bowl in his hand.

"You weren't out very long. You should rest and regain your strength. Here, eat this." He said as he gave me a bowl of stew. I took a spoonful of it. This was the best food I had had in weeks. I ate so fast that I nearly got my tongue splintered from the wood of the spoon.

"Where are the gods?" I asked. This question appeared to take him by surprise.

"The gods?" He asked with a smile. "And which gods would you be referring to?"

"The ones who saved me from the wolves. I was crying, ready to die, and fire came from the sky and got rid of the wolves. You must have heard it, the fire made a loud shrieking sound as it came to earth."

He just smiled at me as he stood up. He was very tall, six feet at least. He went to a bowl that was sitting on the table. He filled it with water and soaked a cloth in it. He brought it back to my bedside, wrung out the cloth and put it on my forehead.

"Well son, it's not often that I'm mistaken for a god," he said as be brushed a long lock of red hair from his face, "and I thank you for the compliment."

I became very confused. I had seen and heard things come from above to defend me.

"How could you have saved me? You're just a man."

Upon reflection, I can't think of anything that I could have said that could have sounded less grateful. He just continued to smile.

"You were right when you said you saw fire, but you were too scared and tired to see anything else. I was standing over you clubbing the wolves away with a heavy piece of wood. I had lit the end of it to scare the animals. Wolves hate fire."

"But what about that horrible screeching? Neither man nor wolf makes a sound like that. And whatever it was, it was cutting the wolves to ribbons."

He stood up and headed into the next room.

"I won't be a moment," he said as he disappeared through the door.

He came back a moment later with a very large and angry looking bird clinging to the thick glove on his left arm.

"This is David, my falcon." He stroked David's head as he spoke. "He got his name because he is generally more than a match for anything far larger then himself. If you don't believe me there are about a half dozen wolves out there that can testify to that fact."

The angry looking bird let loose with a yawn. My savior put a hood over the bird's head and placed him on a perch by my bed. This made me a little nervous, but I kept it to myself.

"As for me," he said, "my name is Rik, and I'm very glad to meet you."

He looked expectantly at me. I figured that was the point where I was supposed to tell him my name.

"Why were all those men hanging from the yard arms of the Mist?" The question took him a little by surprise.

"Those men were involved with a mutiny aboard that ship. The captain and local navy conducted a house to house search for all the men. I believe they got all of them but five. Why do you ask?"

"It was the sight of all those dead men that scared me into the forest." Technically speaking, I was telling Rik the truth.

"The ship I was on with my parents sunk about ten days ago and I swam to this shore about a week ago. I have been stealing food to live ever since. I figured those hanging men were thieves and I didn't want them to kill me too."

At this point, I left the realm of technical truth and wandered into the land of bald faced lies.

"By the way, name is Hakon." I put out my hand in a gesture of friendship. I saw no sense in giving him my real name, especially when they are still looking to hang me for mutiny. He smiled and took my hand.

"Well Hakon, you are more than welcome to stay with me for a while, as long as you are willing to earn your keep."

The offer sounded too good to pass up. For the first time in weeks it appeared that things were going my way. I nodded in acceptance and started looking around his keep. I was in a large central room with a hearth and pot of stew cooking over it. The walls were of cut stone with a high ceiling. Weapons were hung around the room as decoration along with many antlers. There was a long table and doors to other rooms at both ends of the north wall. The bed was out of place here. It was more than likely set here for my benefit. This room had all the trappings of a man who had money. Unfortunately my survey of the room brought up one thing missing.

"Rik, where is your alter to Odinn?"

"Why do you ask?"

21

I conducted myself like a coward when the wolves attacked, I need to ask his forgiveness or he might send me to Niffelheim."

"And this is a bad thing?" Rik asked.

I was shocked. How could any man in our day and age be ignorant of the ways of Odinn?

"Niffelheim is a horrible place where cowards go. Once there, your soul gets eaten by a dragon and you are dead forever," I said, "only the brave and strong can go to Valhalla and be with the gods."

At that moment I realized why I landed here. Odinn has brought me to this place to educate this man in the proper ways of worship. Who knows how lost he may be?

"This is very interesting Hakon, what happens in Valhalla?"

He sat there looking very interested indeed, so I continued.

"Once a warrior has made it to Valhalla he becomes one of Odinn's soldiers. He fights battles all day to amuse Odinn. If he is killed in one of those battles, the warrior is resurrected that night to feast with the gods and ready himself for the next day's battles."

"And this goes on for the rest of eternity?" He asked.

"Of course not," I said, "in the end there is a war between the gods, Odinn's army, that would be us, and the enemies of Valhalla. These would be Loki the trickster, Jormungand the world serpent, Fenrir the great wolf, Hela and her army of undead, and the fire giant Surt. The gods and those who served them taste a final death in that war along with their enemies. The world will be burned and reformed. New races of Gods and humans will inhabit the earth and start their own cycle."

After I had finished with my brief explanation about our religion. I awaited a response from Rik. He sat in thought for several minutes, pulling at his chin in the same manner one with a beard would. The longer he thought the more confident I was that I had converted him. The minutes plodded on. He still sat and thought. This is not unexpected, he appears to be about thirty so it stood to reason that it could take quite a while to undo many years of wrong teaching, perhaps as long as an hour. If that is what it would take, I was willing to sit and wait. After about fifteen minutes, he stopped thinking and started talking again.

"If I'm a bad person or a coward I go to Niffelheim and my soul gets eaten by a dragon and I experience final death and become non-existent. Do I have that part right?"

I nodded in agreement and he then went on.

"If I'm brave and good I go to Valhalla and spend my days fighting and dying for another being's entertainment and I eventually get thrown into a war in which not only do my gods get killed but I also die. This is a final death and I am then nonexistent. Is this also right?"

I started feeling sick in the pit of my stomach. I nodded to him in agreement.

"That is the most tragic and futile belief I have ever heard of. No matter what you do it ends in death and nonexistence. No wonder so many of your heritage and generation seem so aimless. They have nothing to look forward to. It is really a shame, all they have to live for is the day."

He then put another blanket on me, wished me goodnight and smiled as he left.

As I write this, I can't describe exactly what I'm feeling. Part of me feels like I have somehow played into his hands. My mother used to do things like that. When I argued with her, she made me describe my position and hoped that it sounded just as ridiculous to me as it did to her. For the most part I feel ashamed for even momentarily doubting what I know to be true. I will explain to him again tomorrow. I think I can make him understand it properly next time.

23

Chapter 4

"Hakon, get up! Your breakfast is ready."

I was in a state of half sleep when I first heard the call. The noise wasn't enough to raise me from slumber, but unfortunately it was enough to mess up a rather good and exciting dream. It was the type of vision that I hadn't seen since my experience with dead herring, so many months ago…and I had planned to enjoy every minute of it. The naked English women had returned and were happily frolicking on a white sandy beach. Their frolicking turned to wrestling. They tumbled to where the water meets the beach and continued their mock combat in the mud. The wet sand clung to their bodies in a very complimentary fashion and I could no longer stop myself from joining in the fight. I grabbed the blonder of the two and wrestled her to the ground. The other had given up the idea of combat and proceeded to massage my feet. I had maneuvered myself to a position above the blonder one and was preparing for the "pin" when I heard the merciless bellow from Rik telling me it was time to eat breakfast.

At that moment, my dream took an uncomfortable journey downward and slightly to the left. Instead of pinning the chesty Brit woman, I was in a romantic embrace with Rik, as David, his falcon, bit and clawed at my feet. I woke with a scream. I wiped the sweat from my brow, dressed, and went to breakfast. I decided that at some point in the day I would have to make time to update my journal. The details of the wonderful dream so viciously and prematurely taken from me would have to be written. Perhaps if I refer to the good bits before bedtime, I will be able to start the dream anew.

From the day my mother gave me this journal, it has been my constant companion. This book has been to Hel and back with me. It was stuffed down my trousers when I hid in the herring barrels and as I ran for my life into the forest after Bjarni's massacre. In fact, throughout all my adventures, I have never lost sight of it. With that in mind, it is almost silly how often I lose it in my room. Perhaps if I picked up the clothes or made the bed every now and then it would help my organization of things. But I will ponder that another time.

Rik smiled at me as I sat down to breakfast. He learned long ago that it was better for both of us if he did not know about the kind of dreams that make me scream.

"Hakon, after breakfast, I want you to go into town and pick up some seed. The ship should have come in last night and we can't risk letting it sell out before we get our supplies."

I paused for a moment and then I realized he was talking to me. I know I was the only person in the room, but the clouds in my morning brain were still mixing with remnants of my delightful dream so it took me a little while to comprehend anything. On top of that, I am still not used to being called Hakon, even though I gave myself that name.

"I'm sorry Rik, I guess I am still dreaming a little. What did you say?"

"I could have sworn that horrified scream from your room signaled the end of your dreams for the day." He said with a laugh.

He continued to chuckle to himself as he went for his purse. I was certain, that once again, I was the butt of one of his many private jokes.

"Here is some silver. We are going to need plenty of seed for the upcoming planting season. Take the wagon and make sure you feed the horse before you leave."

With that, he took his bow and falcon and left for the hunting grounds. I followed his instructions and fed the horse, hitched her to the wagon, and headed into town.

I don't go into town often. In fact, I have avoided it as if it were a leper colony because of my fear of being recognized and wanted for my participation in the mutiny on Bjarni's ship.

I stopped the wagon when I got to the top of the hill that overlooked the town. Hvarf, as the city came to be known, is the closest thing to real civilization we have here in the colonies. It is a sprawling harbor settlement that is just lousy with merchants of every sort. You can't swing a dead chicken in Hvarf without hitting someone who wants to sell you something. Dozens of wooden lodges dot the countryside below. Most of these are either shops, or belong to those who owned the boats that are our lifelines to the outside world. I flipped the hood of my jacket up onto my head and headed down into the town.

I kept my head slightly down so that my facial features were not recognizable. Between that and my hood I believed I was safe. Actually I was probably being a bit over cautious. To my knowledge, Bjarni had not been seen in town since soon after he murdered his crew. Even so, there is nothing wrong with erring on the side of caution.

The guards at the gate gave me little notice and I passed through Hvarf's defense wall without resistance. Once inside, I got the same locked in feeling I always get when I'm here. The wall that surrounds this town is here for a very good reason. It keeps Hvarf safe from raiding parties. It is large, gray, and very foreboding. It dominates the view from inside the city, and completely blocks out the landscape. To me, this makes the town feel very cold and lifeless. I also have the fear that the wall that locks out danger could very well lock me in against my will.

Today Hvarf is sprawling with activity. A ship came in last night and the supplies she brought have replenished the city. Considering the fact that the boat is docked in the harbor, outside the sterile walls, they must have unloaded in record time.

Going through the city, I can find just about everything for sale. On this day, it took me a while, but I finally made my way through the mire of over eager merchants and found the man selling wheat seed. As I waited my turn to buy, I glanced over to the booth across the road. Despite the festive atmosphere the supply ship brought with it, that place was as cold as the walls that surrounded it. The obese man, who was apparently the proprietor, displayed his wares in front of the stand. Six women and two children sat there, with leashes around their necks. They were dressed in tattered rags, and were covered in dirt and bruises. Most of them had red hair. My assumption is that they were captured in Ireland. I could verify this if only I could have had a good look at their faces. The Irish have such distinct facial characteristics. But they each kept their heads down, like beaten dogs. The portly man who owned them leered at me from behind his dark unkempt beard and puffy face. I got my seed as fast as I could and left. I certainly didn't want to end up on the sales floor with those poor Irish people.

The money Rik gave me for the seed was about double what it actually cost. This is not the first time he has overpaid. I used to think he was trying to test my honesty by seeing if I would give him the money back. But the first time I tried to give it to him, he refused it and said that was my pay for doing my chores. I wasn't about to argue with him.

I started wandering through the town, looking for something to waste my money on. Perhaps a pair of boots, or a jacket. I could always use a new hat or some gloves, or perhaps I should think of something less practical. Then I thought to myself, I could pay a visit to Madam Grunnhilde. I have heard many rumors about how impractical spending my money there would be. I have also heard that the women she employed could, for a small price, make all my fantasies about English women come true. Would Rik approve of me going out whoring? Probably not, but who in the world would ever tell him?

I congratulated myself for this wonderful idea but then my left eye caught a glimpse of something sparkling in the sunlight. On display in front of the blacksmith's shop was a beautiful sword. The blade was thick, double edged and over a meter in length. The hilt was bound in leather with a round pommel. The price of that very fine weapon was just under the amount of money I had in my possession. Perhaps I had enough to buy that and visit Madam Grunnhilde's. It took not another moment's thought. I gave my money to the blacksmith and took possession of my new weapon. As I held it in my hand, I suddenly understood why the sword is so important to our gods. In an instant, I had incredible power! I could easily kill. I held life and death in my hands. I was a god!!!!

I held the sword up in the air and as I reveled in my newly discovered omnipotence. I walked directly in the path of a man preparing to mount his horse. As I bumped into him, I looked him in the eyes and in that instance I was stripped of my newly acquired magnificence. I dropped my sword and fought back the impulse to cry. The man bent down, picked up my sword and looked at me as he said, "Did you drop this?"

It had been over a year, but one does not forget the face of Bjarni Herjolffson. So, he hadn't left the island...or...maybe it was his ship that brought all the supplies to this colony. Either way, both thoughts were a ridiculous expenditure because they were to be my last.

"You should be more careful, son. You might accidentally hurt someone."

Then he took a cloth from his jacket, wiped the dust from my new sword and did the unthinkable. He handed it back to me. I looked at him with eyes as wide as the gap between my upper and lower lips. He broke into a smile and winked at me. Then he mounted his horse and rode away into the crowd of shoppers and peddlers.

I wasn't sure what had just happened. All I knew was that he had me dead to rights and he let me go. Rik would have called this divine intervention from his god. At that moment I would not say he was wrong. I can also say that a very big weight has been lifted off my shoulders.

Chapter 5

It was a little over two months ago that I turned thirteen. Rik said it was always his family's tradition to ask god for something on your birthday. I just shrugged my shoulders, closed my eyes, and asked what I thought was an imaginary and silly god for something I wanted very badly–deliverance from the lie that being a wanted mutineer forced me to live. I liked Rik, he was very, very good to me. I wanted to tell him everything. He gave me a roof, food and a sense of belonging, and I couldn't even tell him my real name. So this is what I asked his god for. I went so far as to tell him that if he granted my wish I would confess everything to Rik. After my birthday was over, I didn't think too much about this pact. My disbelief in Rik's god's ability to act stemmed directly from my disbelief in Rik's gods ability to exist. The events of yesterday however proved me wrong.

It wasn't a classic smiting, like the ones that Rik reads from his bible. After all the stories I had been told, I really expected a more exciting deliverance. In the old days, this god used fire from the sky, vindictive foreign armies, frogs, boils, angels of death, and some really nasty weather to protect those people who called upon his name. In my case he seemed content to use a simple change of Bjarni's heart. A turn of the cheek, if you will. I have often listened to Rik read to me from the bible. In the old days, his god was a fire and brimstone, a "kill them all and I'll sort them out later type of guy."

For a while, I began to think we were worshipping the same god. There are definitely some Odinn-like similarities in that thinking. But then as that book drones on, it gets into all this "love your neighbor" and forgiveness stuff. And now he solves my problem with

Bjarni without bloodshed. Oh well, Rik's god seems to have calmed down between testaments.

Regardless of the dull nature in which I have been saved, a deliverance is still a deliverance, and a promise is still a promise. I will now, grudgingly, admit that Rik's god probably exists. Because of this, I now have to keep my word to him and tell Rik everything.

When I had arrived home from my trip to town, the house was empty. Apparently Rik was still out hunting with David. I used the free time wisely, and began rehearsing my confession. I started out by genuflecting. I perfected the most pathetic manner possible. I prepared to distance myself from Rik's reach, yet close enough to kiss his feet if necessary. With my head bowed, my eyes wide and pleading, slightly tear filled and peering upward, I knelt with my left knee pointed toward Rik and my right knee only partially resting on the ground. My hind end would be toward the door. That way I could beg for forgiveness yet still be out the door in seconds should my plea be denied.

I removed some of the heavier objects from the room. We certainly wouldn't need the frying pan or his hammer in the room for this discussion. I just put them somewhere safe where they could not be quickly or easily found.

I started to feel bad about the preparations I had made for Rik's return. Over the course of the past year, he never raised his voice to me, let alone made any move to hurt me. Then again, I had never given him any cause. Most of what I told him were lies...but they have been so very endearing lies that he has had no reason to see me in any light other than the eager, appreciative, good boy that I have told him I am.

I went into my bedroom and prayed to Rik's god. I figured he helped me with Bjarni, perhaps he could keep Rik from getting too mad at me. I told him that I was happy here and that I didn't want to leave yet another home. It was about then that I heard the door open.

"Hakon," he called, "come help me clean these rabbits."

I stopped, mid prayer and went downstairs.

"Hey, you got some nice fat ones." I said as I looked the rabbits over.

"We can make a pretty hearty stew out of these," he said while handing me the knife.

"Mmmmmmmm, rabbit stew will be a good change. It has been weeks since we have had anything but fish," I said as I cut out the rabbits' innards.

It had been a pretty long time since I cleaned something without gills. I could feel my stomach making room for the feast I was soon to enjoy.

"So how was your trip into town?" Rik asked as he pulled the skin off one of the rodents.

I began to sweat a little. I would have to tell him soon or I never would.

"Not bad, I got the seed, and something else."

I took a deep breath and grunted as I began to flay the meat from the bones. I had forgotten how bad these things smelled when you opened them up.

Rik smiled, "Well don't keep me in suspense, what is it?"

"It's in my room," I replied. "I'll go get it."

I pushed away from the table and ran to my room. Rik always insisted on seeing everything I bought for myself. He told me he needed to inspect all my purchases to see that I wasn't cheated. But I think he just likes seeing me get excited over the things I buy.

I handed the sword to him. He looked it over carefully. He ran his hand against the steel blade and then held it up to the light. He was looking for flaws in the metal. He rotated it in his hands to check it for weight and balance. After his inspection, he turned to me and said, "Is this a hint?'

I was a little taken aback at the question, and gave him a rather confused look.

"Well you bought yourself a sword and now I expect you need someone to show you how to use it."

He had that same father and son project look in his eye that my father used to get when the roof needed repairing.

I nodded as he handed the sword back to me. I really did need someone to teach me the finer points of sword fighting. My mother would never allow me to learn, so I was at absolute zero as far as knowledge of how to use this weapon.

"Well, if we're going to turn you into a swordsman, there is no time like the present to start. Let's see your form."

Rik went outside and came back with a thick fire log from the pile by the door. He propped it up on its end and put the rabbit I was just about to clean on the log.

"All right, we'll start with something simple," he said. "Imagine that you are all that stands between this vicious rabbit, and his goal of world conquest. And the only way you can stop him is by chopping off his evil head."

I grabbed my sword with both hands and stood a pace away from the target. I raised my weapon, closed my eyes, and brought the blade down with all my might. Unfortunately, it was a bit too much might. Not only did I completely miss the rabbit, but my grip slipped and the sword went flying from my hands. It imbedded in the hearth wall, within a feathers length of a very startled and angry David. Rik went over to David and literally smoothed some ruffled feathers.

"Maybe we should start tomorrow, outside, far from other forms of life," Rik said as he smoothed David out.

I pulled my sword from the wall and went back to my rabbit gutting.

"Oh, Rik, something else happened today. I met up with a man who no longer wants to kill me."

I had decided to scrap the worship/forgiveness approach and, instead, just inject my confession into casual conversation. My hope was that I could undermine the seriousness of the topic that way. Rik just sat there with his arms crossed and looked at me. This is how he showed me he needed more information. Also the look on his face was such that he was not going to discuss this in a casual manner.

"Yeah, this guy, Bjarni, wanted to kill me, but he doesn't anymore. I guess he's calmed down over the last year. That was when I made him angry, last year…uh, this was before you and I ever met."

Rik's arms were still crossed and his eyes kept staring, all I could do was keep talking.

"...uh, yeah, I was kind of on a ship before I came here. It didn't exactly sink the way I told you...but me and the crew were starving and angry and there was this sort of um...mutiny. I wasn't part of it. I just stood and watched most of the time, but I am sure everyone thought I was part of it. They killed everybody else and I kind of wound up here. When I told you that my name was Hakon, that wasn't the whole truth. I had an uncle who used to call me Hakon, but he was a little confused in general. Anyway my name is Harald and I'm sorry for lying. I just didn't want to get hung."

Rik uncrossed his arms and stood up. It looked as if he had grown six feet taller. He walked over to me and put his hand on my shoulder. My first action was to cover up. My first thought was regret that I wasn't genuflecting as I had practiced. Then, he spoke.

"It's about time you told me."

I uncovered and gave him a look that could only be recreated with soggy potters clay.

"The news of the mutiny was all over the island. Soldiers came to my home looking for you and any other mutineer they could find. When I found you, you were haggard and nervous like one on the run would be. I'll never forget the way you flinched when I picked you up. You looked like a fish just thrown into the boat. Physically, you fit the description and the unimaginative story you gave me was only one a desperate mutineer could tell. Who else could you have been?"

My face was still contorted into a mask of confusion.

"If you knew all this time, why didn't you tell me?" I asked

"I was afraid you would just run again. From what I saw when I met you, survival was not your strong suit. I figured you would tell me when you were ready. Until then, I knew I could keep you safe."

I was intoxicated with relief. Now that the lie was over, I had no idea what to do. I have no means or desire to go back home. I have lived the life of a man and I cannot retreat to the life of a boy, the youngest of thirteenth sons. Rik seemed to know everything else, so I decided to ask him.

"Rik, what happens now?"

He sat back down in his chair and picked up his knife.

"We continue cleaning these rabbits," he said, "and I stop calling you Hakon."

Chapter 6

I spun away just in time to watch Rik's blade slice the air where I used to be. I swung my sword in a circle from my right side, around behind me, to the left. Rik's weapon met my blade before it could possibly inflict a wound upon him and then he was back at his relentless attack. Rik's style of fighting was based upon intricate patterns of spins and footwork.

To the casual observer, it resembled a beautiful dance. To the participant, it was a horrifying prospect. At all times during our sparring session, his arcs and pirouettes kept me clumsily off balance. I held my own for quite a while, and then it happened. For one split second, I lost track of which way Rik was spinning and it was over.

I didn't feel the strike to the back of my head so much as I heard it. The sound was like that of a large gong going off in my brain. I began to see small bright lights, like fireflies, appearing and disappearing right before my eyes. The world had suddenly become an infinitely slower and more sideways oriented place. It took me a moment to realize that it was not the world that was sideways, it just appeared that way because my face was pressed against the ground. I vaguely remember saying something about how I was too young and handsome to die, and pleading with god to give me a second chance. I felt the arms of an angel wrap around me and lift me to the heavens. I began to weep for the loss of my young life. At that moment the angel spoke.

"Harald, you're really going to need to get acquainted with your spine if you are going to be any good as a swordsman. For god's sake boy, I barely touched you."

My angel had Rik's sarcastic tone of voice. For a moment I thought I saw heaven, as I was carried down the hill. The sun was glistening and shining off a snow white building. As my vision un-blurred a bit, I could identify the long, sloping sides of the building. It was shaped like an overturned ship. This wasn't heaven...it was home. The sun reflected off the new whitewash that Rik and I had applied last month. What a torturous job that was. The house was at least as long as a ship. Its angled roof made footing nearly impos-sible. I was picking splinters out of my feet for days after. My mind began to cloud again. The blow to the back of my head must have been a terrible one indeed. We reached the house and I could hear the rusting hinges on the heavy oak door squeak as Rik opened it. As we stepped in, Rik accidentally hit my head on the doorway.

"How rude," I muttered as I lost consciousness.

I woke up about fifteen minutes later.

"You're lucky there was no edge on my sword Harald. If that were a real fight you would be dead right now instead of just dizzy."

I felt real lucky at that point. I couldn't think straight and I was certain I would need a whole new head!

"You were doing so well and then it seemed as if you got dis-tracted. All you have to do is work up your attention span, and stop daydreaming about women at inappropriate times and you will make a fine warrior," Rik said.

I could feel Rik's hands on the back of my head. I winced as he touched the damaged area.

"How bad is it Rik?" I asked. "Whatever the wound is, I can take it."

I squinted my eyes and waited for him to tell me I was disfig-ured for life. I would be shunned by women, driven from proper society, small dogs would piddle on me. Even worse, I would have to wear hats all the time.

"Just hold still, you big infant. There is a bit of a bump and a cut back here."

As he said this, I could feel a thick liquid pouring down the back of my neck. It smelled sweet, and had the consistency of watered down honey.

"Rik, what are you doing back there?" I asked.

"It's an old remedy my father taught me, Harald. He used to pour mead over my wounds. It always seemed to help them heal without any complications."

I began to wonder if his father also bathed him in beer when he was a baby. It is a shame that Rik's father died before I could meet him. He sounds like my type of man. Rik rarely spoke of his family, or the shipwreck that killed them as they traveled to Greenland after Rik to colonize. All he would say is that the line ended with him.

Rik put the bottle of mead on the table as he began to wipe the drink off my neck. I had never had the opportunity to try mead, or any other type of intoxicating drink for that matter. Well, never as long as you don't count fermented herring juice. My mother always insisted I was too young to drink anything of that nature. Even at the mayday celebrations she would only allow water or fruit juice. Then I came to live with Rik and I have never even seen him take a drink. I had resigned myself to a torturous life of clear-headed sobriety; that was until I realized that Rik stocked some of the gods' liquid. I looked up and muttered a quick "Thank you" to god and then made a grab for the bottle.

"Are you sure that your father didn't mean that you were to put the drink in the wounded person instead of on the wound. The acts are kind of similar, and I can see how something could get lost in the translation."

I grasped the bottle as I said this. It was a smooth, ceramic bottle. I felt better just having it in my hands, I couldn't wait to see what I would feel like when I had downed the entire bottle. I lifted the open mouth of the bottle to my lips. I could taste the residue of the mead that had just been poured on the lip of the bottle. I closed my eyes, ready to accept the sweet liquid onto my tongue and suddenly it was wrenched from my grasp. I opened my eyes to see Rik putting the cork back on the container.

"This is not for children." He said as he gave the cork one more push.

"Then we are lucky there aren't any in the room now."

I puffed out my chest as hard as I could as I said this. Perhaps if he noticed my hulking frame he wouldn't see me as a child and then he would give up the bottle. Being a generous sort, I was prepared to split it with him.

Rik cast that all too familiar wicked little smile of his.

"Oh, you're a man now then. Forgive me for not noticing."

He gave a little bow as he said this. There is a fine line between patronization and flat out sarcasm. He didn't even bother to straddle it. He fell clearly on the sarcastic side.

"I guess a man like you can handle a drink then, huh?"

I gave him a slow defiant nod. I was not going to back down to him on this one.

"Well then, I suggest we celebrate your virility by a good old fashioned day at the pub. What do you say?"

"Do you mean it, Rik?" I said hopefully.

"Of course I do. Go clean up and we'll head into town for a few drinks."

The sarcasm in his voice had disappeared and he was all smiles. I ran outside to the shed to make room in my bladder for the night's activities. Once relieved, I went to my bedroom to find suitable attire for the afternoon's activities. Minutes later I emerged from my chambers in black trousers, my favorite leather boots, and a hooded shirt of purple cloth. I fastened the ties in front on my shirt as I sped through the house. Rik had saddled my horse and had her waiting outside the door.

"Ready Harald?" He asked.

What a foolish question, of course I was ready. We took the road to town at a brisk trot all the way. I was so excited I couldn't speak on the way. Rik was basically quiet and just smirked a lot.

We rode into town and came up to the saloon. For the first time, I didn't feel like a prisoner inside the protective walls. After hitching our horses, I grabbed Rik and dragged him into the pub. Upon reflection, I think I may have been a bit over eager. I looked around the place and found that it was not much to look at. Its wood plank walls were plain with the exception of the chunks that were taken out of them at certain points. I could make any number of assumptions on how the blemishes got there. As long as most of my guesses ended with a drunken brawl, I probably had a pretty good chance of being correct. Other than that, it was essentially a wooden box. On the walls, I could see the outlines of where weapons had once hung for decoration. I can only guess as to why they were no longer there. Probably not a good idea to have weapons handy in the middle of a tavern brawl. The barkeep was standing behind a long counter. He had a large number of barrels stacked behind him. These were presumably filled with the liquid that I so badly craved.

We chose a table in the back corner of the pub and Rik went to get our drinks. He returned with two frothing horns of mead. To my extreme surprise, he handed them both to me.

"Rik," I asked, "which one do you want?"

It didn't matter in the least to me which one he took. They both looked equally good to me.

"That's all right, Harald. I'll catch up to you later. Those are both for you."

His tone was almost challenging, daring me to finish off both of the horns myself.

I examined the one in my right hand and sucked the foam head into my mouth. It was sweet and tasty. I brought the lip of the horn to my mouth and poured the liquid down my throat. To Rik's surprise, I didn't stop until it was completely empty. I lifted the now empty container high, threw back my head and let the last pearls of liquid drip into my mouth. Once finished, I slammed the drained horn, mouth first onto the table. I looked defiantly at Rik as the bull's horn curled upwards from the table, standing as evidence of my manhood.

I would have loved it if an artist could have captured the look of utter and absolute disbelief on Rik's face at that moment. I smiled at Rik in almost a predatory way and glanced at the mead in my left hand. I quickly drained it in a similar manner. I sat there for a few moments afterwards. I was thinking, very smugly, about how I had just demonstrated my manliness to Rik. I remember thinking about

41

how I was willing to keep up that pace all day, so long as he continued to stay in shock. I remember wanting another drink, and then I remember losing consciousness for the second time that day.

I'm sure for the next several years my actions will become part of the folklore of that tavern. Hearing the information from Rik secondhand was nearly unbearable, thank god I don't actually remember anything. I guess it started with a spontaneous and unsolicited speech during which I spewed my hatred for the Danes and blamed them for years of petty wars, the death of many good Norwegian men, and the low birth rate amongst Rik's cows. I suppose thinking about the cows made me sad, because I was told that I sat on the floor and cried for a half an hour while chewing on a bar rag.

As the story goes, I then stood up and literally buzzed around the bar like some demented humming bird. After which, I tried to wrestle a dead mouse from the barkeep's cat. After losing to the cat, I sauntered back to my table and announced, to several of the tavern's patrons, my undying love, devotion, and gratitude for their friendship. It all ended when I put a small cooking pot on my head and suggested we take Madam Grunnhilde's by force and carry away the women. On that last point, I got rousing support from some of the pub's drunker customers. Our crusade made it as far as the door. That is where I collapsed for the rest of the day…and night…and part of the next day.

I woke to the sound of wardrums. I was afraid to open my eyes for fear of seeing whom I had offended. I put my hands over my ears to deaden the noise, to no avail. The drums were in my head. They were joined by some boats, those annoying fireflies, and some overdressed English women. I opened my eyes only to see more fireflies congregating on my bedroom ceiling. I closed my eyes and they followed and began to buzz around the inside of my eyelids.

Regardless of what I did, I was stuck with them. I resigned myself to this fate and began to give the flies names. I did this alphabetically. I had just reached the name Baldar, when I was hit by an overwhelming wave of nausea. I focused to keep my mouth closed as I groped for something, anything to empty myself into. I reached

42

onto the floor and grabbed a receptacle, and then proceeded to get very sick into it. I caught a glimpse of my choice, and immediately began to lament.

Even with my blurry vision I could see that I had grabbed one half of my favorite pair of boots. I was about thirty seconds into my mourning when another wave crashed into me and I was forced to ruin the other boot. I laid back and figured I wouldn't sit up again until I was sure I would ruin no more footwear. Rik entered the room with a bowl of broth. Every footstep sounded like a hammer striking an anvil.

"How do you feel?" He asked in a voice that was not unlike a thunderclap.

"I think I'm dying." I said.

I rolled over and saw my boots laying on the floor.

"My boots are already dead, I think." The remorse in my voice was almost impossible to hide.

"Well you're going to need to get better for tonight." Rik said as he felt my head for a fever.

I looked at Rik with concern as he said this.

"We had such a good time last night that I think it would be a good idea for us to go back."

The mere suggestion of going out for another night at the pub was enough to make me go hunting for another shoe to ruin.

"Uh, Rik…" I said. "I think I'm done drinking for a while."

My stomach made a sound in agreement.

Rik smiled and put a cold, damp cloth on my forehead.

"That's fine Harald, it's not that important."

He tiptoed out of the room and left me to rest. I have never suffered to that degree in all my life. I wished for death. I was certain the barkeep had poisoned my drinks. This sickness could not be normal. I raised my eyes to the ceiling and tried to see through the fireflies. I remembered that whenever I had called upon Rik's god, things seemed to get better. I closed my eyes and prayed for him to take away the sickness. I promised that if he did me that favor he would no longer be "Rik's god" to me, I would call him my god. As I prayed,

43

a calm settled over me. My eyes closed and I fell into a deep peaceful sleep. I am amazed that God even watches out for the drunken idiots of the world who call upon his name. When I awoke, in a very private and personal ceremony that involved nothing more than a quiet field and Rik's copy of the Bible, I renounced all things odinn.

Chapter 7

This was supposed to be the cultural and spiritual high point of my life. This experience carries the same nostalgic value of a first step or word. Thirty years from now, I should remember this day with a big silly grin and an obscenely embellished story. All I wanted was the excitement and celebration that generally follows the discovery and use of a new bodily function. None of that was to be.

If things had gone as planned, I would be reliving the memory of writhing around in a soft bed with a naked English woman. Instead, the only image that comes to mind right now is that of me sitting in a mound of mud with David, perched upon my head, gripping a pink piece of undergarment in his mouth. I know it was pink, and I'm certain it was an undergarment because it draped down from his mouth and covered the entire right side of my face. It was my vain hope at that moment that it would hide my face just enough to prevent future identification. In reality, I'm sure the streak of pink in front of me just emphasized the fact that I had absolutely no dignity left. Oh well, what good is dignity? It won't serve as my ticket back to Madam Grunnhilde's. For, as of today, I have the dubious distinction of being the only person ever banned for life from her whorehouse. I'm fifteen years old and at this rate, it appears I'll be stuck with my virtue for the rest of my life.

The day started out in a grand fashion. As Rik headed for the fields, I told him I was taking David hunting and that I would be back in few hours. Since Rik would be gone for most of day, I had all the time in the world to do what I pleased. I checked my purse to make sure I had enough money. For the past several weeks, I have sort of exaggerated how much my trips to the market were costing. Rik never goes to town so I figured he had no way of knowing I was skimming some money. We got our supplies, Rik got some change (just enough to show him I was learning the negotiation skills he taught me) I kept some money and we were all happy!

Sometimes, I have felt guilty about my little crime (God says what I am doing is bad) but if Rik paid me the proper allowance, this wouldn't be necessary. I figure I'm worth at least ten more silver pieces per week than he is paying. At least the stolen money is going to a good cause. Occasionally, Rik sits me down and tries to teach me effective bargaining skills. It is his hope that these lectures will bring down the cost of my shopping trips. This is the last thing I want at this point.

I put on my leather hat and went off to get David. Several months ago, I tried to teach him to sit on my shoulder. He stayed for three seconds and decided it wasn't for him, and then promptly took residence on top of my head. I made several unsuccessful attempts to break him of this. No matter what, though, he decided that he liked it on my head and that was the end of it. Rik had suggested that it may be a nesting instinct and perhaps a comb and haircut would solve the problem. Personally, I like my messy blonde hair just the way it is. It is warm in the winter and makes a very nice pillow when I take outdoor naps.

Anyway, I'm keeping my hair so I must also tolerate David nesting on my head. I'm willing to wager that I look silly enough to inspire a new trend and in six months every one will be wearing falcons on their heads.

I had a day to myself, a purse full of money, a falcon on my head and I was looking for trouble. In particular, the type that involves naked English women. I went to our herring barrel and took a few big sniffs before leaving. It doesn't have the same effect on me that it did when I was twelve…so very long ago. I was sad, for a second, to discover that I had outgrown one of my more decadent pleasures…reliving the indecent, dead herring inspired hallucination of frolicking with naked English women…

I started to hitch my horse Storm, given to me by Rik on my 14th birthday, to the wagon but it was just too much work. So, I gave up on the idea of going by wagon and proceeded to saddle her. I tried to buckle the saddle but my hands were shaking so much that I couldn't. I had heard that the finest English women are available on a first come, first served basis and I simply had to have the best of the lot. So, in my haste, I just forgot all preparations, jumped on her bareback, grabbed her mane and rushed to Madam Grunhildes

I tried to make Storm rear in a dramatic motion. I figured this would be fitting considering the importance of my mission. I pulled back hard on her mane, kicked her sides and prepared for her to stand and whinny. Instead, she just turned her head toward me, gave me a look and started back towards town. This horse was a gift from Rik on my fourteenth birthday. More often than not, this animal treated me as if I were the one who was presented to her as a present.

Apparently, Storm didn't understand what was going on. I needed an appropriate send off, for I was on my way to losing my virginity. Well, I wasn't actually losing it. To lose it suggests that it was either going to be stolen from me or I would accidentally misplace it. It could never be stolen because I had a purse full of money and I was eager to buy. I wouldn't have misplaced it because I knew in advance exactly where I was putting it and I had fond thoughts of being able to go back and visit it now and again. Regardless, this was a very serious matter and Storm should have recognized it. I wanted a dramatic movement and, curse it all, I was going to get it.

I pulled back on her mane again and kicked her a little harder. She stopped and looked at me in a most angry way. She scraped the ground with her foot. I watched the long hair around her hoof sway as she moved it. She dug her foot in, flexed the muscles of her back and in the process, caused my legs to spread even farther across her back. For a moment, I worried about an injury that would ruin my day. She started walking again. I was enraged at her disobedience. I pulled her mane as hard as I could. She went up. Unfortunately, it was not the front end and I had suddenly found myself flying through the air. I landed on my rear end, but the ground did not hurt me upon impact. I seemed to land on something soft. I lifted my head in time to watch Storm galloping toward home. I also saw David perched on a branch of a nearby tree. He appeared visibly shaken by the ordeal of being thrown from a horse.

As I stood up, I caught a whiff of a horrible odor. To my horror, it was me! My landing was cushioned by the droppings of the last horse that had passed by. I smelled terrible. Yet, I could not waste any more precious time worrying about such trivia. I was on a mission. I whistled for David. He took his place atop my head and I started a brisk run for town.

It took me over an hour, but I had finally arrived. As I approached the threshold, I realized paradise was only a few short steps away. I knocked on the door and was invited in by a beautiful, smiling, sable-haired woman with an English accent. As she took my coat, she spoke.

"Welcome, my name is Fanny and..."

The smile left her face and she took several steps back.

"What in the king's name have you been rolling around in?"

The combination of horse droppings and sweat from my run here had left me a wee bit more pungent than I realized. Apparently, she was not the only one to notice. A loud, shrill voice came from a room in the back.

"What died in our lobby?"

A matronly, walrus sized woman burst from the room. She was obviously in charge. My only guess was this was the famous Madam Grunnhilde.

"Look boy, we appreciate our customers coming in clean."

She looked me over like I was a pastry or something.

"You're new here. Fanny, go give this boy a bath and anything else he can afford."

I eagerly took Fanny's hand and followed her upstairs. As we were ascending the stairs, I heard Madam Grunnhilde shout some other instructions.

"Charge him extra for the bath and make sure he takes that ridiculous falcon off his head."

We arrived at the bathroom. A pair of large men were bringing heated water from downstairs. As they were preparing my bath, I heard the slamming of a couple of doors and some angry voices. A few minutes later, Madam Grunnhilde burst into the bathroom.

"Will you clean this bastard up? His stench is affecting business. Two people have left because the smell has taken them out of the mood. And will you please remove that stupid bird?!"

She made a sudden grab for David. That was a bad idea. Sudden moves around an animal that is naturally nervous is a good recipe for disaster. David flew up and started flying amok in the bathroom. Madam Grunnhilde tried to catch him. She stood on a chair and stretched out to reach him each time he passed by. Her long, dark hair flung around her head whenever she clamored to grab him. From David's perspective, he was being annoyed by an unfamiliar predator...probably a cross between a flying rabbit and a human rat.

David perched himself on a high cabinet and then dove for her hair. It was a perfect attack. His talons grabbed the swinging hair and to the surprise of all, it came off. Madam Grunnhilde grabbed her bald, exposed head and started screaming. David was not through with her, however. He dove at her yet again. She avoided him, lost her balance and fell in to the bathtub.

"Get that brat out of my place!" She screamed.

As a pair of burly men threw me out, I heard her threatening to kill anyone who let me back in. And so, for the second time in one day, I flew through the air and landed on my hind end in something soft, this time, a thick mushy mound of mud.

I sat where I landed. For a moment, I worried about David and what they might do to him. Then, I watched as he burst through an open window. He flew to me and took his perch upon my head. In his mouth, he had Madam Grunnhilde's pink undergarment. I don't want to know how he got it. I just want to forget this day ever happened. Truth to tell, the only way I will is by figuring out another plan to get back in.

I took my time as I walked home. Thoughts and plans of getting back within the walls of paradise consumed my mind. Like many heroes of the past, to get to the good stuff I had to defeat the ugly, hideous dragon. The good Madam is probably much more round than most of the world's dragons, but her surly disposition more than makes up for the fact that she is lacking the size, scales, and pointy bits that most dragons have. Her breath is much more insidious than traditional dragon's fire. Instead of instantly reducing you to a pile of ash, and sparing you the actual pain of entering the heavens, the acrid stench of her breath simply lingers in your nose until you want to throw yourself off a very high cliff. In other words, she will be a most formidable dragon to slay.

I was so wrapped in these thoughts that I barely noticed the strange horse tied to the post outside our door. In all the time I had been here, Rik had never really had a social caller. My first thought was to sneak around to the side window, and peer in. The thought did not last long in my head. I wasn't overly bothered by the idea of spying on him, (perhaps I should have been, but I wasn't). But, considering the long walk I had just completed and that my soft bed was just a mere stride through the house away, I decided that I would simply walk in.

They didn't notice me immediately. It took their brains a full two seconds to register my presence in the room. Once they had, their immediate reaction was not unlike a pair of children getting caught showing each other their private parts.

Rik had a stunned look upon his face. It was not a normal stunned, but rather the type of stunned that one gets when he is handed a live weasel and told to stuff it in his pants. His companion got over his initial shock rather quickly, and struck a more relaxed posture. He leaned back in his chair, and began to drink at his horn of mead.

"So this is the young fella you have been going on so much about Rikky boy," he said with a lilt in his tone.

He was trying to hide it, but he had the accent of a Dane. How dare a Dane show his face on these shores! Considering how hard and brutal the Danes have been to just about every other race in the north, how dare Rik let him in this house!

He stood up and put his hand out. He was tall and very lean. Not skinny, just lean. I guess the polite thing to do would have been to shake his hand. I was not feeling especially polite, and just crossed my arms.

He smiled at me, and continued to hold out his hand.

"C'mon lad, I don't bite," he said.

His smile grew wider and stretched the skin of his weather beaten face. On the surface he looked friendly enough, but God only knows what evil skulks in the heart of this Dane.

"That's not what I heard about your countrymen, and if half of what I know is true, biting is the least of your crimes," I told the scum as indignantly as possible.

He began to chuckle, then his mouth opened into unbridled laughter. The Dane then dropped back into his chair heavily, put his feet up upon Rik's table, and took a strong pull from his horn of mead.

"Rik, I salute you. You have trained this fine young man to recognize an enemy when he hears one," he raised his horn to Rik as he said this, and snarfed into his glass as he tried to drink and laugh at the same time.

Rik had regained his composure, and was busy wiping the area of the table around where his comrade's feet now rested. He was noticeably annoyed by the dirt that had fallen from the Danes boots and onto the table.

"He may remember the sound of an enemy, but it seems that he has forgotten his manners. Harald, this is Ulf. He is an old shipmate of mine from our time in the navy, the **NORWEGIAN** navy," Rik had a definite bite in his voice as he said this.

"Don't be mad at the lad Rik, he is only doing what is right. Snubbing me for the Danish scum I am," Ulf's laugh had a way of filling the room. He wasn't fat enough to have a laugh that big.

"Harald, I am a Norwegian through and through, but my mother was Dane. Growing up around her I seem to have picked up some of her accent. Don't worry boy, you are not the first to make this mistake," Ulf leaned over and slapped my back so hard it knocked some of the mud off my shirt and back on to the table where Rik had just cleaned.

Rik gave me a look of annoyance, and began to wipe where the mud had landed. I knew this man, and he was disappointed with me for not accepting Ulf's hand when he offered it. I knew I was going to get a lecture about this later, but I did what I could to make the situation right. I mumbled an apology to Ulf, and put my hand out for him to shake. He took it heartily and just kept laughing and drinking.

When he finally released my hand, I went out back and got cleaned up. The rest of the evening was spent in my room listening to the muffled sounds of conversation and laughter. I know that Rik is an honorable man, but I can't help thinking there is something more going on here. I shall have to keep a closer eye on Rik in the future.

Chapter 8

According to the chapter, *Revelations,* in the Bible, something called an "Anti-Christ" will rise up on the earth. He will be responsible for tribulation, plagues, and generally mess up the world for the rest of us. The story does not tell of this demon's origin, but it is my opinion that this monster will be from Denmark. Only a Danish person could be so careless. The Danes had spent the last several centuries doing their best to make life miserable for anyone who wasn't one of them. For years I have heard the tales of Danish warships appearing on the horizon of some unsuspecting Norwegian town. The attackers would silently anchor their longboats off the shore of the doomed settlement. It was always the same. The early morning calm would be shattered by sounds of a host of warriors dropping into the water as they came over the sides of their boats. Your mind starts to register what is going on when you hear the steady, fast footsteps and sounds of jingling chain mail as they come for you in a dead run. Before you can even react, your door has given way to the assault of a Danish boot. If you are lucky, you are killed.

It is far worse for those who live. The women are subjected to the pain and humiliation of being raped over and over. In my nightmares I would see the poor, unfortunate men who had not been instantly killed. Tied to a stake, they would be the offering in the Danish sacrificial fires. The death would be slow and horrible as the flames began to sear their feet and grow, fueled by their bodies, until pain or death took consciousness from them. Afterwards, other survivors are taken away in chains and sold as slaves. With that in mind, it is not difficult to understand why I get defensive when Rik starts keeping company with a man who has the accent and smell of Denmark.

Rik never explained his friend as anything but an old navy buddy. On the occasions when I pressed him for details of their relationship he would just smile, muss my hair, and tell me I was too young to hear such bawdy stories. I have real problems envisioning Rik doing anything that would be the least bit immoral. I closed my eyes and tried to imagine him seriously drunk, committing crimes against nature, and getting dangerously mixed up with the type of women that his mother would have nightmares about. All I could see though, was him trying to convert the pagan masses as he traveled around. If given a bland brown robe, and a tasteless haircut, Rik would easily qualify as a monk. Regardless of this, I still have the nagging feeling that there was more going on that day than just lighthearted reminiscing over beers.

Rik sends me to town on a pretty regular basis. I make sure that these trips are now as short as humanly possible. I no longer take the time to window shop or stare longingly at Madam Grunnhilde's. I get back home as soon as possible in an attempt to see who else Rik invites over when I'm not there. I have yet to catch Rik with any other visitors.

Yesterday as I was coming back from town, I passed a messenger coming from the house. I hailed him, but he ignored me and kept moving. I shouted at him again and he took his horse from a walk to a gallop. I decided to forget him and get home as swiftly as I could. I urged Storm on a bit faster. She gave an angry grunt, but complied. When I got home Rik was saddling up his horse.

"Harald, I'll be in town for the next few hours," he said, "Can you watch over things while I'm gone?"

I nodded yes. He smiled, patted me on the back, mounted his horse and left. The light smile that usually graced Rik's face was replaced with a very stoic expression. I wasn't sure, but I thought I could feel his hands shaking as he patted me on the back. This, combined with a mysterious messenger and Rik making a sudden, rare trip to town, was too much for me to ignore. I could not, in good conscience, entertain the notion of staying home.

I unhitched the wagon from Storm and pushed it into the barn. I left the supplies of grain, fruit, and corn on the wagon. I was pretty sure it would keep just as well there as it would in the root cellar.

I ran from the barn to Storm. I tried to mount her without breaking from a run. Many were the times I have seen Rik use this trick to get atop his horse. He would run, leap, and be on his horse in one fluid motion. There was enough room from the barn to Storm for me to get up to full speed. I leapt at what seemed to be the appropriate time, plated my hands on her lower back to catapult me to what I was hoping would be the saddle. I guess there was a slight speed miscalculation. I vaulted over the saddle and slid down her neck. She had lowered her head to eat. I hit the ground hard on my backside. The impact was felt over my entire body. I had to check my teeth to make sure they were all still there. I guess David heard the sound of a mistake in progress and assumed I was home. He flew out of the house through an open window and dropped down right in front of me with my leather hat in his beak. I put the hat on and David took his place atop my head. I mounted Storm in the normal fashion and followed Rik's trail to town. My hope was to shadow Rik, unnoticed.

I reached the point where I could follow Rik without raising suspicion. From this distance, I just looked like any other rider heading for town. Well, I would have if not for the falcon on my head. It didn't really seem to matter. Rik never looked back. He may have been preoccupied with whatever the messenger had to say to him.

About ten minutes out from town, the sound started. It was unmistakable. Music, laughing, singing, there was a party going on in town, and it was a big one. I urged Storm on a little faster. She gave her standard angry grunt, but obeyed my wishes. As I cleared the treeline, I could see the town. It was nestled at the bottom of the hill. Every house was lit. There were small fires and candles everywhere. I could see the townsfolk making merry in the streets. They were dancing to the music from a number of musicians who had taken this occasion to ply their talents. From my perch, atop the hill, individual sounds were indistinguishable. It was all just one loud, happy noise. Something had happened, and everyone felt good about it.

I continued to follow Rik. After entering the gate, he stopped a couple of times to talk to the townsfolk. He would lean down from his black Arabian, and the person he spoke to pointed in a direction. Rik kept following the pointing fingers of the citizens until he reached a clearing on the far end of town. In the center of the clearing was a huge bonfire. There were people dancing around the bonfire, despite the lack of musicians in the clearing. They were presumably moving to the leftover music in their heads.

Tattered flags hung in the trees around the bonfire. They bore the distinctive red field and black raven that was the symbol of one of Denmark's nastier raiding parties. Along with the flags, the bodies of dead men hung in the trees. Their hands and feet were tied and they were garbed only in black execution hoods.

I looked for someone who was sober enough to answer some questions about what was going on here. This was no easy task. Eventually I found a heavily intoxicated man who seemed to be less heavily intoxicated than anyone else I had met that night. I asked him what had happened. He looked at me blearily. I tried to make eye contact with him, but his orbs were just kind of floating in the sockets. He pointed in the direction of the trees and let loose with the few words he could still pronounce.

"Raiders…Danish…Caught…Sunk!"

He then laughed hysterically. It sounded like a donkey with breathing problems. He settled down for a moment and took a pull off the bottle in his hands. He began laughing again, spun on his heels and passed out.

I caught a glimpse of Rik staring at the bodies. Even from this distance I could see that he was now in a dour mood. Death was not his favorite thing. To Rik, a city wide celebration over the execution of these men was an abomination, even if they were Danes. Rik turned his horse and left as they started throwing the bodies onto the bonfire. I stayed for a few minutes more. It wasn't long before the scent of burning human flesh began to disturb me. It wasn't like other flesh. It didn't smell like rabbit or pork. It was acrid, and slightly sweet. I thought that I would enjoy seeing this happen to our enemies. Instead it just left me sick.

I tried to follow Rik through the crowd, but it was so dense and confusing that I eventually lost sight of him. At that point, it didn't really matter. The execution and susbsequent celebration explained the messenger at our home.

I began to feel silly about tailing Rik. Perhaps Rik's friend was just what he said he was–an old Navy buddy who was raised by a Danish mother. And there was no connection between the two events– a visit from a friend and a mass execution of Danes. Rik is far too settled a person to get involved in anything controversial. The more I thought about Rik having some sort of secret life, the more ridiculous I felt.

I was shaken from my thoughts of Rik by the laughter of women. I had been riding around aimlessly as I dealt with my thoughts. My meandering had taken me back to my own personal Mecca, Madam Grunnhilde's. I stopped thinking about how ridiculous I felt, and started thinking about other feelings I was having. I longed to share these feelings with the ladies waiting within. Unfortunately one obstacle barred my entrance to paradise. It was a large and very ugly obstacle. Namely, the one and only Madam Grunnhilde.

When I was last there, I left being the only man banned for life from her establishment. I didn't really have time plan things out. I just improvised as best I could. There was a man passed out in the street. He was still clutching a bottle of wine. I quickly took the wine and poured it over my head. My blond hair soaked up the deep burgundy color.

David was none too pleased about the change and decided to just fly off and angrily circle the building. I figured the wine smell on my hair would probably be no different from that of the other drunks to visit her establishment that night. I was greeted by the same English woman who met me before.

"Welcome," she said as she took my hand, "and what can I do for you this evening?"

Her voice was melodic, and was accentuated by her incredibly charming accent. Her question was loaded with possible answers. Every response I could think of involved more of what she could do *to* me rather than *for* me. All the words tried to come out of my mouth at once. Despite the number of suave and sophisticated lines I could think of that would have this women swooning, the only word I could muster was, "Kaplatic."

She giggled at my stammering, and took my money. Fearing that another nonsensical word would escape my lips, I conducted the rest of the transaction in silence.

"A quiet one, eh," she said as she took my hand, "I like a man who doesn't feel the need to bog down the act with senseless conversation."

She led me upstairs to the bedrooms. Madam Grunnhilde was patrolling the hall, putting her ear to many of the doors. It was nice to see that she was interested in whether or not the patrons were enjoying themselves. Once we got upstairs, she came over to give me a customary greeting. She looked me over before speaking.

"Have you been here before, boy?" she said with a hint of menace in her voice.

I vigorously shook my head no. She gave me an even closer look. My mouth felt as if it were stuffed with cotton. Speaking was out of the question.

My Englishwoman handed her my money. She counted it in front of us. When she was sure that I had met the price, she escorted us down the hall. She stopped at a door closest to the back stairway, and fumbled through a ring of keys. She cursed as she tried one key after another in the door. This went on for several minutes. I could feel the nervous energy of anticipation filling my body. I was nearly ready to break the door down myself when she finally found the proper key.

"Have a goooooood time." She said in a sarcastic voice as she slammed the door behind us. And presumably continued her door inspection.

Our room was small, but tasteful. It had a pair of candelabras on either side of the door. There was a table at each side of the bed. A single candle sat upon each of the small round tables. The walls were painted an off white and the curtains were of a see-through fabric. Pink linens on the bed matched the pink curtains. Our bed was against the wall opposite the window. On a good night one could probably lay in bed and gaze at the moon. Astrology was not my top priority that night, though.

"My name is Fanny," she said as her blue robe fell to the floor. It bunched around her ankles as it hit the floor.

Her hair was sable in color and the loose curls fell delicately about her shoulders. Her high cheek bones were accented with rouge, as were her lips, but she wore no color around her blue eyes.

Fanny shook the robe off her feet as she walked over to the candles. She lit a small stick with a lantern that was sitting on the floor. Her left hand cupped the candle as she applied the burning twig to the wick. I watched intently as she did this to each of the four candles. Candlelight danced and played about her body. It cast shadows on her pert breasts and washed over her softly banking hips. her legs were long and muscular, with small, delicate feet finishing off the package.

I moved in closer to her. I kissed her fully on the mouth. I think it was good as far as first kisses go. I would say she tasted like wine, but I'm sure that taste was just my hair coloring dripping down into our mouths.

I closed my eyes as I ran my fingers through her hair. I was so enraptured with her that I barely noticed the sudden whoosh of air that came in through the window. For a brief moment I considered closing the window, but that would mean freeing myself from her embrace. The window could wait.

She undressed me as we kissed. Her fingers were moving up and down my back as she maneuvered me to the bed. She brushed a dark feather off the pillow and continued kissing as we lay down.

"Ummmm...you're a hairy one aren't ya?" she said in a soft seductive voice.

This took me a bit by surprise because I'm not hairy at all. In fact I can't even grow a beard, let alone any on my back. At that point I realized that I could no longer feel her hand upon me. I took this opportunity to finally find my voice and speak to her.

"Fanny," I said with slight alarm, "I'm not sure where your hand is, but it's not me you're feeling."

Her eyes widened and her body tensed. She tightened her grip on whatever she was feeling and brought it up into the candlelight. It was a very large, very dead, rat. It had the distinctive claw marks of a kill by a bird. David launched himself from the ceiling beam where he was perched and snatched the rat from Fanny's hand. At the very least, that explained the whoosh of air I felt.

Fanny screamed and bolted for the door. She swung it open, knocking Madam Grunnhilde, who was listening outside our door, down the stairs. I ran out of the room. Madam Grunnhilde was on her back at the bottom of the stairs. She stared up at me. Madam Grunnhilde had a sudden flash of recognition.

"YOU!!!!!" She shouted.

That was all I needed to hear. I slid down the rail as fast as I could. That was a bad idea considering I wasn't wearing any clothes. The friction burns on my private parts will take weeks to heal. I dashed to Storm, this time successfully leaping on her back from behind, and galloped away. Behind me I could hear Madam Grunnhilde threatening to kill me if I ever darkened her door again.

I was about a mile down the road when I felt it was safe to take Storm out of a dead run. I dismounted her. My escape had left the inside of my legs chaffed and the bouncing motion of the horse had bruised other things I prefer not to mention. At least I'm alive. I wouldn't be if the Madam had gotten her fat little hands on me. David settled on my head as I began my long journey home. He again had Madam Grunnhilde's undergarment in his beak.

Rik was asleep when I came in. I dressed myself in my night-clothes and went to bed. As I laid there, staring at the ceiling, I wondered how I was going to explain my absence to Rik. He will certainly ask why I was not home. As my mind travels from one thought to another, explanations to Rik have melted away and schemes of getting back into Madam Grunnhilde's are beginning to form.

Chapter 9

I shaved again this morning. I scraped the knife carefully across my soapy face. Afterwards, the blade revealed the same thing that I have seen for the past several months–clean white soap, and nothing more. I would say that my facial hair had deserted me, but desertion implies that there was once a presence.

It may be seen as strange for one who is trying to grow a beard to be shaving. In reality, I'm trying to train my face. My older brothers believed that if you scrape the fuzz off, it will grow in a bit thicker. They all eventually went on to grow mighty beards. My experience to date shows that the act of shaving has scared off the real hair. Apparently I have missed something they have done.

I could waste no more time thinking about my non-existent beard, Rik was taking me to my first Thing, and we were running late. I wiped the rest of the soap from impotent face and went to my room to finish dressing.

I remember my father talking about going to Things in our region back home. They are supposed to be meetings to discuss topics of the day that pertain to the well being of the community. Things also serve as a way to communicate the needs of the people to the local rulers, and through them to the kings. For as far back as anyone can remember, the Thing has been our people's most important tool in the shaping of the policies that rule our lands. In reality, the meetings my father went to primarily involved drinking heavily, secret handshakes, hired girls, and really big hats. According to Rik, that was no way to hold a responsible Thing.

Looking back, I don't remember my father ever even pretending the Thing had anything to do with responsibility. Rik assured me that this region took their meetings seriously and that important ground was going to be covered. I found that kind of disappointing. My father may never have had any influence over the direction of the country, but it usually took a full week to get him to stop smiling. Now that is what I call a productive meeting.

I pulled a white wool shirt over my head and let it fall loosely over my torso. I then fastened my sword belt around my waist and brushed some dust from my black trousers. I looked in the mirror one last time. My hair hung messily about my shoulders. I pulled it back and tied it with a piece of leather string to neaten my appearance. With this done, I went to the stable to meet Rik.

We had a good hour's ride ahead of us, and I dreaded the thought of listening to him drone on the entire time about the history or importance of the local Things. So as soon as he said, "You know, Harald, Things are a very important part of our heritage," I pulled my sword and smacked his black Arabian, Rachel, across the rump with the flat of my blade. She reared and went galloping out of control ahead of me. Rik wheeled and came back at me with his blade. He made a wide arc with his sword, and missed me by several feet. I started to laugh at him, but then a fairly large tree limb came crashing down upon me. It effectively knocked me from Storm's back and into the dirt. We spent the rest of the ride in mock battle and short races. I was actually sorry when we reached the Thing. I was having such a good time on the ride, I didn't want it to end.

The meeting was held in a large open field. A bonfire burned in the center and torches lit the perimeter. There were probably about two hundred men within the encircled area. Most were in small groups, engaged in what seemed to be casual conversation. Others stood alone, trying not to look too awkward about not being with a group.

A man stood upon a rise by the bonfire and introduced himself as Sigurd. He was a very tall and lean man. His thinning brown hair was grayed at the temples and hung down to his shoulders. His leathery face had the texture of the rocky countryside that dominated Greenland. Upon his face he wore the expression of one who had just sucked a lemon.

The meeting started with an invocation to odinn. In less than a few heart beats' time, someone screamed that he was not a follower of odinn. About half the crowd roared in agreement. The other half roared back at them to just shut up and pray. Just then a very monkish looking man stood on the rise, along with Sigurd, and began to recite the Lord's prayer. This, of course, prompted the other man to raise the volume of his prayer. Even by my standards, this was childish behavior. As the prayer part of the meeting became a religious shouting match, I fingered the cross that I wore around my neck. It was an obvious mark as to where my beliefs were. A little voice inside my head beckoned for me to leave it out. Foolishly I listened.

They both managed to finish their prayers and to my great surprise, they did it without coming to blows. For the next hour, there were what seemed to be endless discussions about the region's treasury and what we should do with the money. Their discussion, like the prayer, became a shouting match. It seems that in the adult world it is not the best idea that gets the most consideration, but the loudest one. This explains why so many kings, generals, priests, captains, and wives have such loud voices. It is not that they are any wiser, they can just drown everyone else out until their point of view is the only one anyone ever hears. Whenever I witness adults on their, "Best Behavior," I realize that my facial hair knows better than I. Perhaps it is trying to tell me not to be in such a hurry to enter the adult world.

I stopped paying attention to the meeting when somebody had suggested the money be spent on luppins to beautify the town square. After that I wandered around the crowd and watched people.

I started listening again when they began talking about the difficulty in farming the land they had bought. They were all angry about how they were duped into thinking that Greenland was a lush paradise. A land of milk and honey is what they were told. Most of the land is rocky and hard to farm. Wanting to do something about this was the one thing everyone agreed on. Of course to take action would mean locking horns with Greenland's chieftain, Eirik the Red. Nobody was adamant enough about it to do something that suicidal. In the end, all they really could do was grouse about it. In truth, despite the fact that the farming is horrible, Rik manages to maintain a sizable fortune. I often wondered how he does it.

After what seemed like a small eternity, the Thing seemed to be winding down. I was preparing to make my way back to Rik and Storm when Sigurd brought up one last, hellish topic. He said that we needed to address the Christianity problem in the town. He bellowed about how the Christian doctrine of salvation through belief rather than actions was destroying the very framework of society. How would they motivate soldiers and raiders to action without the hope of Valhalla as a reward for dying in battle? A doctrine of love and forgiveness would put an end to the raids that financially sustain the Nordic lands. It was his belief that Christians should be killed on sight like vermin.

While he was in the middle of his lunatic ravings, the monkish looking man who lead the Lord's prayer got up on the rise. He started to shout about choice in religion and peaceful coexistence. At this point the crowd was becoming more polarized and working itself into a frenzy. People were pushing, shoving and arguing so loud they could barely hear the speaker. As the Christian man was pleading his case, I saw Sigurd, behind him, pull his sword. I screamed for him to turn around, but I could not get my voice louder than the din of the crowd. Sigurd pulled back his blade, swung at the back of the Christian's neck, and separated his head from his body. This stopped the crowd for a moment. His body fell to the ground, yet his heart still pumped blood out the sump that was once his neck.

The next sound heard was the metallic hiss of about two hundred swords being drawn and the deafening clash of steel. I didn't know what to do and before I could figure it out, somebody grabbed the back of my collar and pulled me down. I rolled to my left as soon as I hit the ground. A blade came down and struck the dirt where I had originally fell. I rolled once more and quickly got to my feet to face my attacker. He was broad and muscular with raven black hair and vacant, ice blue eyes. His face was painted chalk white. Presumably to honor odinn as a god of the dead. He wore no shirt. His upper body was covered in thick, dark hair. He was quite a scary sight. He laughed as I pulled my sword from its scabbard. He parted his lips and flashed teeth that had been filed to points as sharp as a wolf's.

He snarled as he came toward me with wide arcing motions. I kept my sword in a tight defense. I blocked his wild swings with the bottom of my blade and angled my sword as Rik had taught me, to nullify the power of his blows. Apparently, the guy was used to frightening his opponents into submission, for he was completely devoid of any technical skill. It was either that or he was simply overconfident. Rik taught me that you only get one chance to surprise someone who thinks you are weaker. You had better make that chance count.

The wolf-man kept swinging and screaming. I kept giving ground. He was making a number of mistakes, but none I was ready to exploit. He took an uncontrolled swing at my head. It was wiser for me to duck than try to block. The force of his swing overextended his body to the left, and opened up his whole right side. I could have killed him, but instead I kicked him between the legs. This way he would be allowed to keep his life and I my innocence.

I turned to run and barely got a step before I felt the tip of his blade cut across my back. I turned to face him once again. My kick hurt him, but it did not disable him. I barely had time to acknowledge the pain of my cut before I was again defending his clubbing swings. He was more wild and angry than before. His attacks came from the left, right, and from above, but never a thrust. He was content to try to overpower me. Also, to this point, I gave him no real reason to defend himself. He was angry, overconfident and determined to kill me. He made an arcing swing from right to left. I rolled headfirst under his attack, finishing my roll behind him. I swung my sword around my body from left to right, and caught him behind the thighs. My blade slashed deeply into the back of his legs. He fell forward, onto his face, and started to grab at his wounds.

I could have left him there. He was crippled and harmless. My back wound throbbed as I felt the blood dripping from the gash. White-hot anger welled up inside of me. I stood over his exposed back as he groped at his legs, and pushed the point of my sword through his back. I felt him shudder as it came out his chest. I slowly pulled my blade from his body and whatever soul was in him convulsed as it left the dead shell behind. I felt sick and invincible at the same time. I was grabbed from behind again and I swung at my assailant. Rik easily blocked my swing. He and his blade were soaked in blood. Rik grabbed my arm, and ran with me out of the battle.

I could not speak to Rik on the ride home. All his talk of self-defense and survival sounded empty. I don't want to know how many he killed this evening. We returned home, and even the mead bath on my wound could not break this feeling of melancholy. I have retired to my room. For now I can only write about this. Perhaps tomorrow I can talk about it.

Chapter 10

It took many days before I ventured from the safety of my room. I just was not ready to face anyone, including Rik. Every night I repeated to myself that it was self-defense. I had no choice. But then the vision would return. My enemy, on the ground, grasping the gaping wounds I left on the backs of his legs. His sword lies at his side. He is defenseless. I could have, should have, just walked away. My anger got the better of me and I took his life. I tell myself he would have done the same to me. I know that without even the slightest shadow of doubt. For some reason it supplied no comfort.

Rik was understanding for the first few days. He allowed me to mourn the death of my enemy without interference. But one day, not so long ago, his patience wore out. I heard his steps all the way down the hall. They were heavier and more purposeful than usual. He knocked on my door once and came in. My sword was in his hand.

The last time Rik had held my sword was on my 15th birthday. He had taken great care to have it forged just for my use. Its weight, its length, all created to be a perfect match to my body and fighting style. It was a gift of love from him to me. The blade was bright and reflected my smile of pure joy back at me. That was then. Rik tossed it on my bed. He looked at me very sternly.

The sword was no longer bright. The blood of my enemy stained its steel shaft. What little reflection I could see was that of a dark and contorted face. The face of one who had taken a life—my face!

"Be outside and ready to practice in five minutes," Rik said.

His voice had no tone when he spoke. For some reason he was deadly serious about this.

I dressed and met him on the hill where we usually practiced. He came at me almost immediately with his practice sword. I dropped my real sword and grabbed my practice sword that was lying on the ground.

Rik spun and arced and struck in that graceful way that usually frustrates the piss out of me, but this time it was a different story. Usually, at that point, my movements were of one trying to duplicate what he had been taught. They were technically correct, but also stiff and lifeless. My encounter at the Thing taught me one very important lesson. It was when I pushed my sword through the body of my foe that I learned it. I could feel him. I could feel what my sword was doing to him. I could feel him shudder as the life ebbed from his body. It was there that I realized the bond between weapon and man. My sword was no longer a lifeless piece of metal. It became an extension of my hand and my will. It was as much a part of me as the mind that moved it. To Rik's disadvantage, it was a lesson that I had learned well.

As I swung my weapon through the air, I no longer fought its momentum. Instead I moved with it, creating spins and arcs of my own. My movements were similar to Rik's, but still very distinctly mine.

For the first time in all my sparring, I had my teacher giving ground in his own defense. I continued with a furious onslaught, giving him no time to consider a counter offensive. We locked up for a moment. I looked at Rik, and noticed he was panting from the exertion. I took full advantage of the split second he allotted me while he caught his breath. I brought my right leg up and kicked him backwards. I followed him with a forward roll. The somersault carried through as I rolled to my feet. I used the momentum created by this motion to lend extra strength to my sword as I struck down. Rik had his sword up in defense, but to no avail. A loud metallic snap was heard as my weapon came down across his blade and snapped it at its midpoint. The blunted end of my sword came down heavy upon his chest and sent him crashing to the ground.

"You're dead," I said in a monotone voice.

I contained the temptation to laugh or do a little victory dance. I wanted to stay mad at him for dragging me out here.

Rik pushed my sword away. If we had been using edged weapons instead of blunt practice swords he really would be dead. This didn't seem to phase him. He got to his feet and calmly brushed himself off.

"Do you feel better?" He said as he picked up what was left of his weapon.

"Wha…" I said, more than a little confused at the question.

I never expected to ever beat Rik, but the few times I thought about it, it wasn't like this. I figured he would be a bit angrier, and claim he let me win.

"Do you feel better?" He said again with a little half smile on his face.

I thought for a moment. For some reason I did feel better. But, I felt so guilty I wanted to spew out my innards. I dropped my sword and started to tell Rik everything I was feeling. This was the first time in days I had really talked at all. I told him how I killed the man when he was already beaten. Even worse, I never gave my enemy the chance to repent to God for his sins. A soul is in hell and it is all my fault.

Rik told me that there were no magic words he knew to fix how I was feeling. In his opinion, that man chose his own path when he picked the fight. We stopped and prayed to God for forgiveness of my sin.

Rik confessed that he forced me outside to practice because he was afraid I would become too withdrawn. He wanted to give me some time to sort it out for myself, but when I had stopped communicating entirely, it scared him. He knew the physical activity would do me some good. Rik knew that the sword practice would bring my feelings about that fight to the surface. Almost like a reenactment. No matter what, I still felt guilty. He simply told me to remember the feelings of guilt. They may keep me from making the same choice if ever I'm in that situation again.

We walked down the hill to our home. On the ground, by the door, was a sealed letter with some packages lying carelessly about.

They had obviously been set down with the care of someone who knew he was not getting a tip for this.

Along with the packages, there were hoof-prints. The pattern and length of stride of the prints indicated the courier left in quite a hurry. Rik just shook his head and picked up the discarded deliveries.

"I'll bet the courier was no more than seventeen," Rik complained, "only a youth would be so irresponsible."

"And what are you going to do in a year when I turn seventeen?" I said.

I was a little put off at his attitude about young people.

"Well, even though you're not yet sixteen, I already have a plan for you Harald. When you turn seventeen I'm going to marry you off and keep the dowry as rent for supporting you the last several years. After that, you become your father-in-law's problem." He winked at me as he said this. I found it difficult to remain angry at him for any length of time, despite his attitude about young people.

I bent over to pick up one of the packages. I was only half way over when Rik swung his arm straight across my chest to bar my way.

"DON'T!" He said as his arm struck me.

For only a brief second, Rik had a dangerously malicious countenance upon his face. It was gone as quickly as it came. The change was so fast that I found myself questioning whether it occurred at all. Real or no, it is something worth noting and remembering. He quickly put a nervous smile upon his face.

"Please don't bother yourself with this. Weren't you going into town to do some shopping?"

As Rik said this he handed me a small bag of coins. It must have contained five times what he usually gives me. I had made no previous plans of going into town, but I wasn't about to let that stop me.

I grabbed the bag and ran into the house. I rushed into my room, intent on getting on my way before he had a chance to change his mind. I passed Rik on my way out the door. He messed my hair a bit and told me to behave myself. With that I was on my way. I mounted Storm and started her on the way into town.

70

I was about half way there when I stopped and prepared for the night's activities. First I donned a long black wig. My wig was made from the manes and tails of any dark colored horse that had been unfortunate enough to cross my path over the prior few weeks. It was a hairpiece large enough to completely obscure my head, neck, shoulders, and most of my face.

I then tied a pillow to my stomach to change the shape of my body. I covered it with a very large shirt and one of Rik's coats. I had not yet figured out how to explain my sudden weight loss to whichever of Madam Grunnhilde's girls I would draw, but I decided that was a problem best saved for when the clothes came off.

My final act of disguise was to cover my lower jaw with glue and then remove from a small pouch the short hairs from the backs of the same unlucky horses that I took the manes from. I then spread it across my face. This, I hoped, would create a beard and make me completely unrecognizable. My outfit complete, my anonymity secured, I was ready.

I rode into town and up to the front of Madam Grunnhilde's. I knocked and was again greeted by Fanny. She giggled a little, then sweetly introduced herself and led me in. She sat me on a bench in the parlor and said she would be just a moment. She winked at me as she left. For a moment I wondered if she somehow recognized me. But no, she couldn't have, I told myself. It is her job to be charming. The wink meant nothing.

I waited a very long time. After sitting there for what seemed a quarter day, a man came in. He was of medium build with blue eyes and fire red hair. This was not unusual. Medium built, blue-eyed redheads pass through here with the regularity of one who eats too many prunes. What was unusual was that he wore the distinct uniform of the Chieftain's personal guard. A long mail coat, a red cloak, and a sword worn across his back. It was obvious he was not here for fun.

Madam Grunnhilde entered the room. I could feel the hair on the back of my neck beginning to stand at attention. Despite the fact that she repulsed and frightened me, and despite the definite fact that

71

I wanted to be anywhere but near that sword, I got up and moved close enough to eavesdrop on what was being said.

I listened freely. They were too caught up in the conversation to care whether or not someone was there. I listened for about thirty seconds. They then said something that turned my guts to water.

He was alerting her that a man had been murdered by his page in the high country. I could count on one hand the number of people in the high country besides Rik and myself. The guard went on to describe the man's page.

Madam Grunnhilde began to jump up and down, (not a sight I suggest one seeks out), and shout about all the trouble that page had caused in her establishment. I felt numb. I could count on one finger the number of people who live in the high country with a page who fits that description. That would be Rik.

Despite my numbness, I continued to listen about how a messenger watched them fight as he was delivering some packages and a letter. And how he watched the boy strike him down. According to the story, the messenger then ran for his life for fear of reprisal and burst into town telling everyone within earshot.

That explains the dropped packages and that also meant that it was a mistake. He saw our dual and misunderstood the fact that it was just a sword lesson. He must have assumed murder when he saw Rik fall. I began to get the feeling back in my body at that point. It was a simple mistake. I breathed a sigh of relief. Rik was still alive.

As the soldier continued talking, he mentioned how the Governor of the territory sent his private guard to check out the messenger's story. The murdered man was of great interest to Eirik the Red himself. I found this of great personal interest. What connection could Rik possibly have to Eirik the Red? I was shaken from my questions about Rik when I heard the soldier say they found the body of the man. He was run through from the back.

I felt sick. I ran outside as fast as I could. As soon as my stomach was finished emptying itself, I made my way to Storm. I kept my head lowered as I untied her from the hitching post. Not only did I not want to be recognized, but if anyone saw me crying, it might have provoked questions. I was not up to conjuring any stories. I raised my head to mount Storm, and I saw David perched upon the saddle. He was with Rik when I left the house. This eliminated any bit of doubt I had in the validity of the story. He looked at me with his head slightly cocked. He had my leather hat in his beak. I put my arm out for him to perch. He moved off the saddle and on to my wrist. I mounted Storm and started moving for home. I noticed blood on one of David's talons. I wiped it off and examined David for injury. He was clean. Whoever got Rik lost a piece of himself to David.

I rode through the forest instead of the main path. I figured they might be expecting my return. That very possibility cast a shadow over the wisdom of going back in the first place. I knew it was stupid, but where else was I going to go?

I stopped about a quarter of a mile from the house. I tied Storm to a tree and walked the rest of the way. I crouched in the shrubs, a mere stone's throw from our own front door. There were three soldiers standing and conversing. I could hear more soldiers inside ransacking the place. There was no going home for me.

I turned to go back to Storm. I was shaking. My stomach was convulsing. I walked as slowly and quietly as my quivering body would let me. I took a step and could hear paper crackle under my foot. I also felt a solid object as I brought my foot down. I stepped back and saw what I had stepped on. It was the package that Rik had barred me from touching. I picked it up and opened it.

It was an oak box, stained a deep chestnut color. There was a bronze tablet embedded in the lid and inscribed. I wiped my tears and read the tablet

HARALD, ON THIS DAY THAT MARKS THE SIXTEENTH YEAR OF YOUR LIFE, I TAKE YOU INTO MY FAMILY AS MY HEIR AND SON.

It was my birthday present. This is what Rik was so adamant about me not seeing. I wiped my nose on my sleeve, then opened the box. It was Rik's family shield. He had this made for me. It was a little larger than my hand and covered in gold. At its center was a round shield with crossed swords over it. Coming from behind the shield

73

were the spread wings of a falcon. The tip of the wings met a little over the top of the shield. A falcon's head came from behind the top of the shield and pointed to the right. Its eye was a bright red ruby.

I returned this treasure to its box and put it under my cloak. I had my sword, my last allowance, my journal and Rik's legacy. As I write this, I am crouched in the woods at the edge of Rik's property. I have stayed here for three days. I can only think of one thing to do—sell Storm and find passage on a ship. I am still well disguised. I should be temporarily safe. I don't know where I will go, but now I will be satisfied to be anywhere off Greenland.

I take one last look back and one look at the shield and let the tears come. If Rik had lived to give this shield to me, I would have proudly bore the name Riksson.

Chapter 11

Four months ago we entered the year of our Lord, 1000. Many people were expecting plagues, famine and other general bits of nastiness to accompany this new millennium. Some gave away all their possessions and watched the sky, waiting for Jesus to return. For some reason, dates with really big round numbers in them elicit some very unreasonable expectations. To me, dates with round numbers only make the mental mathematics of the events in life irresistible to calculate. My mind went back in multiples of five and stopped on the year that all my wanderings started. It has been a very long time since my mind had wandered back to that time, fifteen years ago, when I was a boy on Bjarni's ship. In fact, the last time I thought about it was in the year, 995. Mental mathematics and round numbers...can't get away from them. It has been at least a ten years since I have had the desire to write in this journal. The news of yesterday, though, warrants some sort of entry. Yesterday was the day that I learned of the death of Bjarni.

For the past several years I have been a hired soldier on the raiding ship, Fenris. We had docked in the Danelaw of southern England late one afternoon. By early evening I was in a tavern working my way to a pretty decent state of intoxication. If memory serves, and in this particular case it probably does not, I was on my fifth horn of mead and trying to figure out this unusual finger puzzle that one sailor had brought back from the far east.

It was rather tube like, with holes at both ends in which fingers could be inserted (into the puzzle, not the sailor.) We sat around drinking and talking of our lives at sea. Actually I remember him doing a good bit more of the drinking than I was. That accursed puzzle had put a death grip upon my forefingers.

"I have been a sailor for nearly twenty five years!" He said in a loud, slurred voice, as he pounded his glass upon the table.

He then got a confused look on his face and started counting on his fingers. This went on for a moment then the confidence flooded back into him.

"AYE..." he said, "Twenty five years!"

He picked up his glass and slammed it back on the table. This gesture was obviously meant as a sign to the innkeeper that his glass needed filling. The innkeeper then slammed his purse upon the oak table to indicate that his wallet would need filling before he would pour another drink.

I ignored this transaction and told him that I had started sailing fifteen years ago upon the Mist with Bjarni Herjolfsson. At this point, I had my hands behind my head, trying to use it as leverage to remove the finger trap. It had been a rather long time since I had a free hand in which to grab my drinking horn, and I was beginning to sober at an alarming rate.

"You sailed for Bjarni?" He said inquisitively.

I nodded as I brought my foot up to my hands and tried to push against my fingers with my leg to free myself.

"He's dead, you know. Fell overboard about a year ago, eaten by squid afterwards or something like that," he said as he stared at the now sitting innkeeper. Their stalemate continued.

My first thought was that perhaps Bjarni had been pushed. His abilities as a captain were the stuff mutinies were made of. I did feel a twinge of sadness as I remembered how he could have had me hung when I was a boy, but instead gave me my life back. By this time my vision was starting to clear. This is generally the final stage before complete sobriety.

I stared a little intently at my drinking companion. There was something on his head. I squinted at it. It took me a moment to realize that what I was looking at wasn't a drink induced vision. He wore a rimmed, purple hat with a big yellow and red feather in it. Until now, I wasn't aware that looking at a hat could hurt my eyes. Well, maybe it was the drink, or maybe it was that the hat was supremely tasteless. Whatever, the hat was not important, nor was the three hundred pound, bald innkeeper sitting across from the hat with a purse and a really, really big knife. What was important was that Bjarni was dead.

To my knowledge, Bjarni had never returned to the new land for one reason or another. He had never gone back and no expedition had made it there yet. A journey of that sort could not go unnoticed. That left me as the last living soul to ever have seen the land to the west. A whole new realm of possibilities had opened up that day.

I remember remaining sober the rest of the evening. In the past I have shown the tendency to ramble when I am drunk, and it was my fear that I would begin rambling about the land to the west if I took anymore of the mead. I figured it was in my best interest if I simply got a room and retired for the evening.

The sunrise in the Danelaw was as beautiful as I have ever seen it. Usually this Island of England is covered in a dense fog. I always figured this was God's way of covering up one of his more major blunders, namely the English. This morning, though, was clear and warm. The sunlight was reflecting off the distant water in a way that actually complimented the usually ghastly English shore. I could hear the bleating of contented sheep in meadows to my west, along with the shrill call of a raven. I got up and looked out the window of my rented room at this spring time scene, and then immediately pulled the curtains.

The sunrise was accompanied by the familiar headache and nausea that always follows an evening of questionable moral behavior. This adds to my normal, morning aches and pains. I also have the ever-present guilt that comes with the knowledge that by getting drunk, I have once again let God down. I'm sure He was not smiling as He watched me play in the mud with the rest of the sinners.

I got down on my knees and buried my hands in my face for my morning prayer. This position serves two purposes. First, it is an indicator to God of how truly sorry I am, and second, it keeps me from having to put out the effort to stand erect and face the morning light. Neither of which I felt up to doing at the moment.

My guilt never lasts very long. My God is a forgiving God, and knows I am not perfect. I will just pick myself up and try to do better next time.

My hangover generally becomes less painful after my morning prayer. I rose from my knees and started to collect my belongings from the floor of my room. I feel fortunate that the innkeeper even allowed me to stay. Especially after he felt compelled to physically throw my new friend and his tasteless hat out of his inn. I guess that is what you get for not paying your bar tab.

My room was small, just four walls, a floor and ceiling, with some hay in the corner instead of a bed. I'm sure the innkeeper had better rooms available, but my association with Rig, the person with the hat, more than likely influenced his choice of the room he rented me. Oh well, at least the innkeeper was nice enough to cut that puzzle off my fingers.

Before his sudden, but expected and airborne departure, Rig and I shared the type of closeness that only perception altering drink can bring on. We laughed, we showed off our scars, we bought rounds for each other. Truthfully, I'm the only one who actually bought a round. Rig just ordered them and then tried to convince our host that we were celebrating a holiday that only applied to our culture. The innkeeper's nationality excluded him from the ensuing merriment of this event. Nonetheless, out of common courtesy he was expected to decorate a symbolic and sacred ewe and give our drinks to us on a two for one deal.

This, of course, left me paying for all the drinks while Rig ordered all the free rounds. In my opinion any holiday that involves me buying all the drinks and worshipping a sacred, decorated ewe is one I want nothing to do with. Apparently the innkeeper shared my sentiment. He promptly and painfully removed my companion from his inn.

Before his removal, Rig and I conversed about our ships. Most of it was the normal talk about captains and crew and who on board might be a homosexual. We also spoke about our destinations. My ship was going on to Ireland and Rig was heading back to Greenland. I thought back to this as I put my possessions in my leather bag.

My thinking was shattered by a large object hitting the window curtains from the outside. I opened the drapes to see David sitting on the windowsill. He gave me one angry screech and ruffled his feathers at me. I petted his head and back until he smoothed himself out. David had a field mouse gripped tightly in his claw. As soon as he was done being angry with me, he proceeded to devour his mouse and I went on to finish stuffing my sea bag. I thought back to the story of Bjarni's death and how I was now the only living soul who has been to the new land.

I finished packing and slung my bag over my shoulder. I put my helmet on and gave a whistle to David. He dropped what was left of the mouse and took his spot atop my head.

My helmet was the ideal perch for David. Its cone shape was easy for him to get his claws around and the leather covering allowed him to anchor himself. Of course it still looked rather silly, but he has done this for so many years that I have stopped caring about how it is perceived.

My first errand was to the Fenris to tell the captain I would not be going with him to Ireland. After that I went to the Sea Dragon, Rig's ship, and secured passage back to Greenland. Once in Greenland, I will work on the task of getting back to the new land.

Chapter 12

"Captain!" a voice called from behind me. The call shook me from my daydreaming and brought me back to my present reality—looking over the side of the ship, Morning Star, as the shoreline drifted by. I leaned against the ledge and allowed myself to rock with the ship. The movement was beginning to lull me back into a sort of waking sleep.

"Captain!!" The voice insistently called again.

I was beginning to think that someone had better damn well find the captain and fast. The twit's constant call for him kept me from my daydreaming. It was also beginning to get on my nerves. At that I remembered that I was the captain of this ship and this kid was not going to shut up until I answered him.

I smiled and continued to look out over the side. I was called for twice; a good captain would have answered him by then, but a great captain would make him call a third time.

"Captain Harald, sir," the huffy little voice said yet again.

This time I turned to see what he wanted.

He was a boy, probably no older than thirteen. I never caught his name; I just called him lad or son, or anything else I could think of for someone who was that young. I straightened my coat before I verbally addressed him, then I folded my hands behind my back. I looked down toward him. He had to raise his head a bit to meet my gaze.

"What is it boy?" I said in the most monotone voice I could muster.

I made sure that at all times I was detached and distant from the crew. A good leader always keeps a bit of a wall between himself and

81

his subordinates. Also, I was not sure what we were going to find in this new land, and if one of my crew happened to have something unfortunate befall him I didn't want to be emotionally attached.

"Well sir," he said. His voice began to crack when he addressed me directly. He lowered his head so that his eyes no longer met mine. I was not sure what about me intimidated him. Perhaps it was my size. I was by no means a giant, but I was one of the rare few to reach six feet tall. Also my years on a raiding ship, and the activity that came with that life, had left me with a strong physique. Maybe it was my mantle of captain that left him feeling insignificant in my presence. It was then that the boy rubbed his eye and then fixed his gaze solidly upon me.

"We have been following the shoreline for some time and many of the crew were wondering when we were going ashore." His voice cracked the entire time.

Perhaps it was the combination of dust in his eyes and his impending manhood that gave my ego the impression that this boy was intimidated. He stood attentively, arms at his side, back straight awaiting my answer. I let him wait for several long moments. I looked off into the sky thoughtfully, then glanced back down on him.

"Tell Rig to dock the first chance he sees a suitable beach."

The boy gave a half bow then went off to give Rig my order.

It was in an English tavern where I first met Rig. Several months ago I returned to Greenland on the ship which he was a sailor upon. He was the first and only person who I confided in about Bjarni's discovery. This close, heartfelt relationship had come only after several drunken evenings together, bearing our souls to one another. Truth to tell, I don't remember much except the drunken part, but according to Rig we had bared our souls to one another. He also mentioned that I had many issues about my mother that it would be in my best interests not to express openly.

Much of what I do remember about our conversations centered around his prowess with women and the fact that he never gave me a direct answer as to why he always wore a hat. When I say "always" I don't mean that he often wore a hat, or he usually had one. I mean that he ALWAYS wore one. Day or night, awake or asleep, he at all times had his head covered. It is for this reason that I never told him where Bjarni's discovery was. All he knows is that I have the coordinates to a great discovery. It may sound silly, but I just can't trust a man who never uncovers his head. It makes me wonder what he is hiding.

Outside the drunkenness, the opinions of my mother, and his mysterious covered head, Rig was also without any money. During the three months that I stayed in Greenland, he had spent the duration sleeping on the floor of my rented room. I always wondered why he had no money. He was employed when I met him, and he had what the Irish call the gift of gab. He could talk his way into nearly anything. It was mainly for that reason that I had let him in on my secrets of new territory. Perhaps the cost of hats was more serious than I had thought.

I had some money saved up, but nowhere near enough to finance a voyage. I needed his skills to help me convince someone with money or someone with power, or ideally someone with both, to finance the expedition.

We got our break when we met Thorvald Eiriksson in a tavern located in the eastern settlement of Greenland. He was very much his father's son. He had the characteristic red mane that earned his father the name Eirik the Red. Thorvald was sitting alone at a table muttering something into a half full glass of mead. He lifted it to his lips and drained it in one motion. He then put the empty glass on the table where there were no less than nine other empty glasses. He apparently had also inherited his father's gift of drinking. My first thought was that if he also had the temper that caused his patriarch to be banished from two countries, we might be in a bit of trouble.

I remember getting up to go to Thorvald's table. I took about four steps and then fell backwards. I had spent the better part of an hour and a half downing beer and mead. I was a little nervous about approaching Thorvald, and I figured the drinks would loosen me up a bit. Unfortunately all that loosened was my knees.

The world around me began to spin as I tried to stand up. I stumbled backwards into my chair, almost tipping the seat and myself over. Then for the third time in my life, I got sick and ruined a pair of my shoes.

Rig grabbed me around the shoulder.

"Harald, what's wrong?" He asked with obvious concern.

He grabbed my face and looked into my blurry eyes. I could see three of him when he did this. Rig smiled a little and released his grip on my face.

"I see you can't hold your drink the way you used to. You ought to be ashamed of yourself." He said wryly.

Rig ordered me some soup. Then he borrowed money from me to pay for it.

"You had me worried there Harald. You just suddenly collapsed."

I drank a little of the broth, and then put my head back down on the table.

"I'm just feeling a little green today Rig," I said as I closed my arms around my resting head to block out the light.

I took another gulp of broth, hoping that a little bit of food would stop the world from spinning around me. At that moment I was in no shape to talk to anybody, let alone someone whom I wanted to convince to give me money. Fast-talking was more of Rig's game anyway so I sent him over to speak with Thorvald.

I kept my head resting on the table, shutting out all light. I kept one ear open, listening for any sound that might indicate that Thorvald had been offended by Rig and was now tying him into one of any number of knots. Somewhere between my growing headache and concentrated listening, I fell dead asleep. I was awakened, some time later, by the sound of a chair being pulled out from under the table and someone sitting upon it. I opened my eyes and raised my head to see Rig sitting there finishing what was left of one of my horns of mead. I rubbed my eyes as he began to speak.

"Mission accomplished," he said as he put his feet up on the table and leaned his chair back on its two rear legs. He took another gulp from what used to be my mead horn.

"Thorvald was very much impressed with your claims about the new land. He has agreed to arrange an audience with our gallant leader, Leif Eiriksson tomorrow at noon. He wants to hear about this new land in detail."

Rig took his feet down from the table and let all four legs of his chair rest squarely on the ground. He leaned in very close to me as he spoke.

"This means you're going to have to part with the location of this precious land of yours." He said this to me in a way that made me want to smack the hat right from his head.

Rig had always made a fairly big deal out of the fact that I would not reveal what I knew to him. He would look at me, crinkle his brow while stroking his long chin, and tell me how unfair it was that I didn't trust him with the location of the new land. It is true, I didn't trust him. It was nothing personal, it was just that this little nugget of knowledge was possibly my key to a far more comfortable future. Deep down I suppose I wanted some of the things that Bjarni was so eager to get once he put his name to the discovery.

Part of me does get some sadistic pleasure out of holding back the location from Rig. I will enjoy seeing his face when he realizes just how ridiculously easy it is to find this land. Fifteen years ago, when Bjarni's ship was lost in the fog, by any logical deduction, we couldn't have passed the southern tip of Greenland by more than a day's sail. We continued west and ran into this new discovery. How could the directions be any easier? Head south from Greenland, then turn west. It will be the first really big land you crash into. But there is no reason for anyone but me to know just how simple it is.

"By the way, I bought Thorvald and myself some drinks and I need you to pay for them." As he said this, the barkeep walked up behind him.

I cannot express how impressed I am with the mold from which God fashioned those who choose barkeep as a profession. One of the most consistent things in my life is that all those who I have met in this field are very large angry looking men. Sometimes they have beards, sometimes they don't. But large and angry are always ingredients in their personal makeup.

I stood up, tipped the barkeep for the excellent service that he had given me and told him that Rig would be taking care of the rounds that he had ordered. I smiled, gave Rig a small salute and staggered out of the establishment. Once outside, I put on my helmet and David dove down and perched upon my head. Behind me, I could hear the faint sound of high pitched pleading and the not so faint, not so high pitched sound of a good thumping going on.

I smile whenever I remember that day. It was not a nice thing to do to Rig, but he was being such a twit he deserved it.

I pushed myself away from the ship's railing. I left docking to Rig. I went back to my cabin. David had been watching my movements from his perch high atop the ship mast. He dove down and through my cabin door as I opened it. Perched upon the back of one of my chairs, he fell asleep.

I didn't have much to do until we docked, so I did something that I have not done in many, many years. I pulled out my journal and started writing. I cannot bring myself to look back upon the earlier entries and the only events of any relevance I feel are the recent ones. The years between entries are just a blur. Coming back to this land I feel the closing of an old circle, I am literally back where I started. Perhaps it is time to start anew.

Chapter 13

I looked very carefully from side to side. As soon as I was confident that nobody was watching, I leaned my head over the railing and spit over the side. The spittle rode the wind and landed gently in the ocean. This was possibly childish and definitely unbecoming to the captain of a ship, but what good is leadership without the privilege of being immature? Well, immature when I feel like it and when there is nobody to witness it.

We were moving so slowly that I could see my spit hit the water. I watched the little ripples that were created by the impact. I turned around and leaned my back against the rail. I watched the activity on my ship. That had a nice ring to it. "My ship." I could get used to that. This never would have happened if it weren't for Rig convincing Thorvald of the potential value of this journey.

After our impromptu meeting in the pub, Thorvald went on to aid us in convincing his older brother, Leif, that it would be in their best interest to support this voyage. Once convinced, Leif went to their father, Eirik the Red, to get him to finance the boat and provisions and hire the men. Leif made a big deal about reminding me as often as possible what a big a favor he was doing for me and how much lobbying he did on my behalf to get the money from Eirik. In reality he probably just asked daddy for a two-week advance on his allowance, and covered the voyage with that. In the end, it didn't really matter where the money came from. All that mattered was that I had my ship.

I mused about the word "Captain." I let the word roll around in my head for a while. It was a role I never saw for myself. I have served on many ships over the years. My status as an educated man

87

had often won me positions of favor. More often than not my talents in reading and writing would place me as the ship's scribe—documenting the exploits of the Captain and crew. Being the leader, the *optimus rex*, was a whole new experience for me. As I watched the activity on board, content that all was going well, a loud voice bellowed my name across the ship.

I forgot to mention one small bit. I may have my ship, but it has a string attached to it. The string is a tall, regal looking man named Leif Eiriksson. His straight, blond hair trails behind him like a cape in a shallow breeze as he strides across the deck. He has the leathery skin of one who spent many a season at sea, and eyes that match the water's color.

Leif was a condition I had to agree to before undertaking this voyage. I was given a ship, the title of captain, and the right to hold on to my secret until we were underway. What I gave away in trade was that a member of Eirik the Red's family would be brought as an observer on this maiden venture.

Leif is Eirik's eldest son, and as heir, had the right to represent the family in this matter. This did not sit well with Thorvald, but there was nothing he could do about it.

Despite the fact that I held the title of captain, and Leif was technically a passenger with no official power, I have never allowed myself to hold the illusion that I am the absolute authority upon this ship. The men may report to me, but it is quite apparent that Leif is my superior. He strode toward me with obvious purpose upon his face.

"Harald," he said in a controlled but powerful tone. "Why have we not put ashore yet?"

His face yielded no expression, but his body was arrow straight and his arms were crossed in a way that indicated impatience. I shifted weight from one foot to the other. I clasped my hands behind my back and stood up straight to give him his answer. I had not really paid much attention to the shoreline as we floated past it. I had put my trust in Rig to find us a suitable place to make landfall. If I was fidgeting, it was because I didn't really have an answer for him. He would not be asking me this question if he were simply in a hurry to get to land. Leif is a widely experienced sailor; he asked me this question because he must have seen something that I had missed. I could simply tell him that I had given that responsibility to Rig, but he would never accept my leaving such important decisions in the hands of my subordinates.

"I have not yet seen what I consider a secure harbor, sir."

Despite the fact that I looked him in the eyes during my answer, I continued to fidget.

"Harald, I have seen at least half a dozen places to land. You are being grossly over cautious. I insist you harbor this vessel at the next opportunity."

With that, he turned on his heel and walked off in a moderate, but purposeful stride. I resisted the temptation to make rude gestures at him as he walked away.

He was wrong, I was not being grossly overcautious, I was being grossly inattentive. There is a difference between the two. Being over cautious implies that I was actually paying attention to what was going on. I could have yelled at Rig and blamed him for the mistake, but the mistake was that I should have been in control from the beginning. I guess there is more to being a captain than just delegating and being aloof.

I kept my eyes peeled for somewhere to land. I spied a cove that appeared to be a decent natural harbor. I shouted the orders to lower the sails and put out the oars. David was perched, atop the main mast and gave out an angry scream when we lowered the sails. Presumably he was asleep and the activity gave him a rude awakening. He dove down from the mast and buzzed Rig, raking his claws against Rig's hat, before settling atop my head. Rig gave me an angry glance. I could feel David spread his wings, readying himself for another attack, but Rig wisely turned away.

For a reason I cannot understand, David has a singular hate for Rig. He barely acknowledges the existence of most other people, but Rig—he despised at first glance. Generally, after an attack, I can see Rig seething with anger. He will start whining and complaining, to anyone who will listen, about his persecution by the bird. When I ask him about it, the vein in his temple throbs and his face turns an amber color. He does a lot of pointing and reenacting of the event. His mouth will move, but he will check himself before he says anything rude about my best friend, David. Even though he whines a lot, to date he never directly asked me to solve his problem with my falcon. I would have expected that he would have begged me long ago to control David. He never did. Instead he just waffles and keeps his head down.

We rowed into the cove and let our anchor down within wading distance of the beach. Leif had us all arm ourselves, go over the side, and wade to land. At first glance, it seemed to be a waste of time for us to come fully armed. There appeared to be no signs of human inhabitants. As soon as we reached shore, Leif took control of the crew. He separated us into three teams. Two to explore the land and one to stay on the ship to serve as a skeleton crew and guard. Each day, team positions would rotate. Leif led one field team and I led the other. We were the only exceptions to the rotation. As the leaders, we were constantly off the ship leading the expeditions.

Each night, upon our return, the men would gather together. They would laugh while eating rations of herring and drinking mead. Leif always ate away from the crew. He at all times kept the rest of us at a good arm's length. He proved to be a difficult man to know.

After about a week, we had learned as much about the lay of the land as we could from where our ship was anchored. The land itself was rather unremarkable. It consisted of flat stone land, and was rather mountainous and glaciered. For the most part it was grassless and barren. Leif named it, appropriately enough, Helluland.

Our investigation did manage to turn up various forms of wild life. A rabbit, evidence of bear, and birds we had not seen before, but we found not even a hint of any type of human occupation. To our knowledge, we were the first people to ever-set foot here.

Leif is not an easy man to read, but one thing was clear to me at that moment, this was not the result he was looking for. Even his stone face could not hide his disappointment. The family of Eirik the Red was very wealthy. Their riches came from a variety of sources, not the least of which was the slave trade. Leif had come here ready to claim the land for his family and, more likely, to scout an indigenous population that he could enslave. Apparently this was one natural resource he was just going to have to learn to live without.

Once we had all made it aboard the ship, we pointed our prow south and continued on our way. We sailed south for three days. As we did, the land seemed to become more hospitable. We landed again on a gently shelving beach with extensive white sands. Leif once again took control and we followed the original three-team plan. This land was starkly different from Helluland.

Where Helluland was mountainous, this area was all flatland. This by no means made our explorations any easier. Instead of having to deal with rocky crags, we had a forest so thick a full-grown man could not fit between many of the trees. Our exploration was slow, as we had to cut our way through most of the woodland. As we got deeper into the forests, we encountered clearings and marshes. It was there that I saw the biggest animal I have ever seen on land.

It appears to be like a deer, but its antlers are broad and flat and much larger. In fact, larger is a good word to use to describe anything about this animal. It has long skinny legs, and a thick muscular trunk. There is a lump at the shoulder, very much like that of a bear. The face beneath those thick antlers is something for which not even the most loving of mothers could find room in her heart. Its snout is long and turned down at the end. The eyes are big, but not as soft as a deer's and menace oozes from every orifice.

When we came upon it, it raised its head to acknowledge that we had entered the clearing, but that was about all it did. One thing seemed apparent; this animal did not fear men. That could mean one of two things. Either it had never seen a man and did not know enough to be scared, or the people of this land kept well away from this animal. I was willing to accept either explanation. Sure it looked passive at the moment. It ate without a care in the world. I am pretty sure though if it became annoyed with us we would probably be in a fair amount of trouble.

91

There was one among us named Sigfried, who was a scribe. I had him write a description of the wildlife we encountered. There was not only this large deer like animal, but we found evidence of large cats, more bear tracks, and a strange rodent like animal with a ringed tail and a bandit's mask. It was hard not to laugh as I watched him wash his food before eating it.

This land was definitely more alive than Helluland had been. Despite that, there were still no signs of man. On our first stop, this did not seem so peculiar. That land was rather barren and inhospitable. Here though, there is land that can be cultivated. The soil is rich and black. It has a good feel to it. There is also food in abundance. Where there is food, man is generally not far behind.

Hunting here is exceptionally easy. It is so easy I feel sympathy for the animals. The birds had never seen a fowler's snare. The small game blundered into the traps like drunks falling over a log. It was just that easy. We restocked our larder with the meat of rabbits and birds. We filled the hold of our ship with the skins of what appeared to be a flat tailed swimming rat. It is an ugly animal but it has a wonderful hide. We could not kill them fast enough. Yes, our luck with the small game was wonderful. Our fortune turned to disaster when we focused on the larger animals.

Olaf the Walker was one of the hands on my crew. He was called the Walker because of his immense girth. He was so heavy that no horse could carry him. Eating was a hobby of Olaf's. It was rumored that he grew his great, black beard just so he could catch the food that fell from his mouth and save it for later. He was definitely not the type of man who could survive on a diet of rabbit and fish.

Olaf went hunting one day...alone. One of his close friends told me that his intention was to kill a deer and surprise the crew with a great feast.

We found his broken body two days later. The ground was littered with the tracks of that huge deer with the flat horns. What was left of Olaf bore the torn flesh and gaping wounds left by that immense rack. Apparently that animal was as dangerous as I had thought.

Olaf was a painful loss for the crew. He had one of those personalities that made him a favorite with everyone. His great girth was often the subject of lighthearted ribbing, most of it inflicted upon himself. He had locked away in his brain a store of bad jokes for every occasion. Even when things didn't look good for the crew, he was always smiling and trying to raise the mood. In short, he was absolutely wonderful for the morale of the crew. Olaf, you will be missed.

Olaf was buried in what was possibly the largest hole ever dug for a human. Leif spoke about how valuable he was and how each of us will carry a bit of Olaf with us for the rest of our lives. We did not leave that place until a proper runestone was erected in honor of our fallen comrade. The story of Olaf the Walker is now written for all time.

Leif named this place Markland because of its dense forests. He also dubbed it an unsuitable place for us to winter. Tomorrow morning, we will be heading south along the coast to find an appropriate place to spend the cold months.

Chapter 14

I woke up several hours ago. No matter how hard I try, I just can't seem to get any sleep. I catch the scent of unfamiliar wood being burned in our fire and look out over a previously never before seen tree line. These things are similar to what I am used to, but still very different. In my mind, this mix of the known and new, coupled with a pinch of the mysterious is keeping me from sleep.

We landed here several weeks ago. We were following the shoreline south from Markland. Our crew, well actually my crew, but sometimes they forget that Leif is not captain, was going about its normal activity of the day. Leif was standing on the prow of the ship, motionless, facing west. He was staring at the passing scenery. I walked up and stood with him. I looked over at his face. To be more specific I looked at his eyes. They didn't blink and seemed as if they were staring a thousand leagues away. He stood straight—with his hands behind his back and bolt upright, as was his fashion. He seemed unaffected by the cold or the wind; he just stood there, motionless, unblinking. To be honest, I hate when he's like that. It is as if his body is with the ship but his mind has gone on holiday and left no forwarding location. He was like this for a rather long while. I was beginning to wonder where his mind had gone, and if it was having a better time than we were. It was just about then that he spoke.

"Land here," he said.

He looked not at me but still continued to stare at the shoreline.

"This is where we shall winter."

He slowly, deliberately raised his hand and pointed to the shore. It was rather unimpressive (the shore, not his hand, though that didn't really impress me either). It seemed no better or worse than anywhere else we had passed during the last several days. Mayhaps, Leif's wayward mind had spent its holiday in the new land and gave him some recommendations on where we could best spend our winter. With a little luck, it found a decent tavern and was well stocked with women of negotiable affection. Once we anchored the boat and waded ashore, we found this was not the case. This land was not necessarily unpleasant. It had a rocky shore that was followed by a long stretch of grass. There were trees in abundance off in the distance.

I assigned a couple of men to guard the ship, and had the rest take up their tools and we all followed Leif. He led us to the tree line. It was then that Leif did something that earned my respect. He took an ax and started to cut away at a tree. He gave no orders and asked for no help. Leif simply found the place he felt was right and started to work on our winter camp. We followed his lead and began to cut logs for our shelters. Leif never backed off from the work required. He worked harder than any single man on the crew. I took note of this and held onto it as a lesson.

Most men I served under were more or less a waste of skin. They treated the mantle of leadership like a reward to be enjoyed, and their crews as a resource to be exploited. Being a leader is more than just being aloof and making dramatic hand gestures. Leif was willing to do any job that he would ask of his crew and because of this, expected them to do anything he asked. He maintained control by example. Perhaps, if I watch him close enough I will learn more.

The site of our camp was some ways from the beach. I didn't like being so far from the boat, but this is where the tree line started and it seemed foolish to drag the logs all that distance just to settle by the ship. Outside of the abundant wildlife, this land seemed to be completely uninhabited. So we believed that our ship was in no danger.

We then cut down suitable trees, notched them to fit and sealed the cracks with mud. Our roofs were thatched with the high grasses that grew in abundance. Most of these lodges served as barracks for the sailors. I, as captain, had my own dwelling, as did Leif. Once finished, our site was aptly named Leif's Budir.

Getting our camp up took us a little over a week. We took a day off to rest our aching bodies and then continued with the task of exploring. It is not as heavily wooded as Markland, but overall it is rather similar. On one of our expeditions Leif found the dried remains of vines. He quickly deduced that these were grape vines and named the land Vinland. I spent the rest of the day arguing with him that we had no idea if grapes grew here and that what he found could have been the remains of one of a hundred different vines. We could have found a vine that no one had ever heard of before. Leif, in his normal stoic manner, was steadfast on the name.

To name the land Vinland implies a land of wine, a paradise. This was simply not the case. I had told him that if this land were ever colonized, people would hear the name and get the wrong impression. They will give up their lives to come to what they believe is literally a Biblical land of milk and honey just to have reality knock them on their backsides. It was just then that reality not only knocked me on mine, but it wiped its boots on my chest as it walked over me. Reality, at that moment, was a very offended Leif.

It was Leif's father, Eirik the Red, who got rich by selling worthless colonies on hard land to people he convinced were going to live in paradise. Greenland is a good example. Eirik founded this land, and named it. He immediately started selling colonies on this new world of Greenland. To look at it from a boat, it appears one is getting exactly what was sold, green fields and good farmland. In reality once you get a little ways past the beach, the land becomes rocky, mountainous and unworkable. Plots of land are allotted based on how much Eirik was given. A better name for it perhaps would be Greyland, or KindaGreenland, or I Broke Another Plow Shear on a Damn Rockland. After a few years, when the land had been developed by the blood and sweat of the colonists, Eirik would again sell colonies, but this time to merchants. They would get the good land and build their businesses, halls and towns. Thus giving Greenland a wealthy upper class with Eirik as ruler, and an entire underclass of serfs to work the land for the merchants.

It was Leif's intention to follow in the infamous footsteps of his father and sell colonies on this land based on a misleading name and what I am now sure are going to be exaggerated reports of Vinland. He had probably written of his accounts on this land before he ever got here.

I would love to do something to somehow stop what I know is going to happen. Perhaps if I were more like Rik I would, but I am not like him. I'm sure that Rik being Rik is what got him killed. While I never heard anymore about Rik's murder, my heart and mind tells me he died defending some principle. I am not ready to put myself in that position. I will sit back, hating what the Eirikssons are doing, while still getting paid by them. If they are going to run this colony gambit they are going to need someone to transport the colonists here. My not liking it will not stop it from happening, and someone is going to make a lot of money. I am ashamed to admit that one of the thoughts bouncing around in my head is that it might as well be me who profits from this. How can I be appalled at what he is going to do, and also be willing to get rich from it? Would my not participating make any difference? This is the type of moral dilemma that generally gives me a headache. I will think about it later, much later.

We continued to explore the land for another week. Our scribes were working extra hours chronicling all the new wildlife that they saw. Regardless of how far out we went, though, we saw no signs of human habitation.

When the snows came, we stopped sending out scouting parties. We instead busied ourselves with hunting and keeping warm. Within our camp, we seemed to have developed two different communities—the pagan worshippers and the Christians. Even though it has been nearly fifteen years since my experience at the Thing, I still can't shake the hate that was felt for the Christians at that gathering. For now all seems peaceful. Perhaps that is due to the camaraderie that they have developed during their time as ship mates, or perhaps my even tempered leadership has something to do with it. Perhaps even more likely, it is just too damn cold to fight. Whatever it is, I thank God for it. I don't feel like a mutiny in my first outing as captain. It does make me think, however, about what will happen if this territory is ever colonized. Hundreds of strangers with no clear direction or leadership. Oh well, not really my worry.

On those nights when I cannot sleep, which at this point is most of them, I leave my lodge and sit on one of the hills facing the camp. Wrapped in a blanket, I like to start a fire and warm a cup of mead. Honey scented steams rises from the cup as I lean my back against the tree and just watch the night until I feel drowsy again. No matter what I do on those nights, I just can't get over the feeling that we are being watched. Sometimes off in the distance, I swear that I see smoke rising from the trees. I know we are alone here. If we are not, we would have surely found a track or a village or something that would bear witness to human habitation. Nevertheless, I just can't shake the eerie feeling. After a couple hours of this, I usually tire and head back to bed as I'm sure will happen on this evening.

My mornings start the same way. Rig pounds on my cabin door. He is now so intolerant of David that he is insisting I do something about his dawn raids. It is no secret that David has never really taken to Rig. I don't have any explanation for that; it is simply the way it is. I don't tie David to his perch. I would consider that cruel. He is a bird and was meant to fly. Usually in the morning hours he gets a bit fidgety and needs to be let out. He goes out the door, I go back to bed and forget about it.

Recently though, he has taken to the habit of buzzing Rig as he leaves his barrack. He will dive at him, full speed, and if he can, inflict a nasty gash. Rig will then come to my cabin, whining about what my bird has done to him and threaten to do some rather perverted and slightly disturbing things to David. I make it very clear that I am sorry for David's poor behavior and promise to try to stop his early morning attacks. I then remind him that harming the captain's falcon is a hanging offense and if any misfortune comes to that bird he will be held responsible whether he is or not. At that point he usually pulls a little on the brim of his hat to cover his reddening face and stalks away to treat his wound.

Outside of minor distractions such as David, or the worry of a pagan/Christian civil war, this has been a very subdued winter. This is a first for everyone here. Generally when we winter a ship, it is somewhere within striking distance of civilization. Wintering can be a rather fun and relaxing time. Now we have rationed and counted everything within an inch of our lives and are all anxiously waiting the spring so we can go home.

Leif is spending most of his time outlining his plans for the new colonies that he will form here. First, though, he is making plans for a few more exploration voyages. I was quite surprised when he told me his plans to extend my tour of duty past this journey. This ship and I will remain as the catalyst of his explorations. Considering our difference in opinions regarding colonization, we shall see what happens when the winter is over and we are back in Greenland.

Chapter 15

Upon the breaking of winter in Vinland, we packed up our camp and made our way back to Greenland. During the voyage home, Leif spoke of little else except the return trip to Vinland and what he wanted to accomplish, which typically makes for good conversation. Leif, though, did tend to go on a bit about it. At one point, I had attempted to change the subject. I believe I mentioned something about luppins and how they tend to liven up even the hideously boring English countryside. Leif then took that opportunity to fill the next three hours with how the luppins would be a welcome addition to the new land and how we should make a point of transplanting some this summer. I suspect at that point he was just trying to annoy me.

I survived the rest of the journey by nodding frequently without adding anything to our conversations. Leif would drone on and I would smile and shake my head in affirmation. This went on until we docked in Greenland. It is there that fate took a hand and ended Leif's luppin planting campaign and all other activities he planned to personally do in Vinland.

Eirik the Red's death came as a surprise to nearly everyone. There is a saying that only the good have the unfortunate pleasure of dying young. If this is to be taken as truth then it was expected that Eirik would have lived to the ripe old age of three hundred and seventy nine. He was an energetic and robust man. He lived life, quite literally, to its fullest. Rumors of how he came upon his unfortunate demise were numerous. Some were fairly believable. Especially the one having him choking to death on the bone of a fowl during dinner. Others not only challenged the bounds of believability, but ran right into those bounds, knocked them over, beat the

ground underneath them and declared the way a toll road. Most of
these rumors included scenes of rather ugly smitings from angry
thunder gods who resented his tolerance of Christianity on Greenland
soil. These explanations for his death were, of course, worth their
weight in dung, but they served to stir up the already anti-Christian
feelings among the populace.

Leif took the news in his normal stoic manner. Any thoughts he
had on the matter were kept firmly to himself. This meant, though,
that he was no longer able to participate in any of the voyages to
Vinland. Now, as eldest son, he had matters in Greenland to attend to
and his official duties took priority over his passion. That passion
being the exploration of new lands. Leif wasted no time in appoint-
ing his brother, Thorvald, to take his place in all matters concerning
Vinland.

Soon after the appointment of Thorvald, Leif traveled back to
Eirik's great hall in Brattahild, the seat of power in Greenland. Leif
carved the rune stone to Eirik himself. He pictured his father's great
deeds and discoveries on the boulder. His craftsmanship in the por-
trayal of his father, the great captain, at the prow of a ship showed
more emotion than anyone ever guessed he had. While Leif mourned
this loss, his brother took to preparing for the next journey west.

It took Thorvald only a month to prepare for the voyage. Most
of my crew had not even recovered from their welcome home hang-
overs before we were picking up and leaving for Vinland again.

Thorvald was a much different presence on board than his
brother, Leif, had been. He was far more rash and impulsive. His
skills as a thinker were definitely in question, but he had inherited
his father's boundless energy. One was not so much awed by him as
bowled over by him. His daily routine was to tear about the ship like
a tornado, forcing himself upon anyone who happened to be there.
One minute you would see him rowing with the oarsmen, the next he
would be adjusting the rigging of the sail, after that he would be
steering the boat.

Thorvald would have been a tremendous help to the ship had
his attention span been longer than that of a gnat. It was not his way

though. He was a man who catered to his whims. As I had mentioned, thinking, was not his strong suit.

When Leif was with us, there was a gap between him and the rest of us. It was as if his body were there, but his essence was separated just by the very nature of who he was. Very much the way some would have considered Jesus. I believe there is nothing so much like God on earth, as an Eiriksson on a ship. Or at least I thought, until Thorvald. With him there was no gap. He was one of the crew, still respected for his position, but still one of them. Most were reluctant to breathe on Leif wrong, fearing a lightning bolt from the heavens would strike them dead. Thorvald would involve the men in games like, "standing blows." The object to this game being the opponent would hit Thorvald in the face as hard as possible to see if he would fall over. If he didn't, Thorvald got to hit his opponent to see if he would fall over.

The opponent usually did. Rig challenged Thorvald to this over and over again. He, of course, never even came close to winning. Most of the time his punches wouldn't even make Thorvald turn his head, let alone fall down. The game settled down to the same repetition. Thorvald hitting Rig and Rig falling down, end of game. It began to get dull until someone suggested that the challenge not be to just knock him down, but to hit him so hard that his damn hat would fly off. To make a long story short, by the time we had to drag the unconscious and battered body of Rig to bed, his head was still covered. Until that night, I didn't think a falcon was physically able to smile.

We followed our original path, and sailed into Leifsbudir. We found that our winter camp was still up, and in good condition. For this reason, Thorvald felt very comfortable leaving a number of men there to continue the exploration of our southern camp, while we took the ship and went north.

We had sailed a full day's journey when it happened. I was at the prow of the boat, attempting to guide us past a rather rocky cape, when Thorvald staggered up to me. In his hand was an empty bottle of mead. Considering the way his body was rocking to and fro I could easily guess where the contents went. He slapped me on the back and let loose with a hearty belch.

"Harald," he said, as I pulled myself up from the deck, yet another victim of one of his backslaps "I'm here to help!"

He took a good long look at the situation. I wasn't about to fool myself into believing that he was actually thinking. I was also not going to be naive enough to believe this man knew the first thing about even the most simple of navigational tasks, among which is maneuvering around obstacles. All that needed to be done was to keep the boat a safe distance from the rocks. In his present condition, Thorvald couldn't accurately judge the distance to the floor. Allowing my ship to fall under his direction would be suicide. I put my arm around his shoulder and spoke in hushed tones in his ear. I did this so as not to embarrass him in front of the crew.

"Thorvald," I whispered, "do you see those big rocks in the distance?"

I pointed to them as I spoke. The look on his face was one of a man who was seeing three of whatever I had asked him to look at. It took him a moment, but I can only assume he chose the one of the three he liked best, and then he pointed to it. He huddled closer and matched my whisper with equally hushed tones.

"Yes, yes...I see them quite clearly. Hela has put these rocks in our way to stop us, but by all that is holy we will get past them."

I was less worried by the fact that he was seeing supernatural conspiracies than by the fact that he was pointing a frightening number of degrees to the left of the rocks. In reality he was pointing to a clump of trees just past the beach. Thorvald then stood as bolt upright as his current level of alcohol would allow. He stood at the prow of the boat and pointed his empty bottle to the wind and yelled.

"Oh rocks from Hel, you will see the sons of odinn prevail this day. Make ready to be passed!"

I quickly turned to shout the proper order, in the hopes that I could get it out before he said something we would all regret. I felt a very strong hand cup my mouth and before I could break free of its hold I heard him bellow...

"In the name of great odinn, steer hard...um, hard...go that way!"

He pointed in the direction of the clump of trees he had mistaken for the rocks.

I broke free of his grasp and shouted the order that would take us a safe distance around the rocks. My men did not comply. As far as they were concerned a member of the Eiriksson family had given the order, and that was gospel to them. I was a captain, the Eiriksson's were kings. My word was secondary.

I ran to grab the helm myself, but it was too late. I heard the sickening crack of wood being splintered by stone. My ship bucked as though her back had been broken. The prow rose out of the water as we collided with the rocks. Most of the crew braced and took the hit with the ship. Our cabin boy went careening across the deck. He tumbled uncontrollably and it was obvious that he would not be able to stop himself before he went overboard. I dove across the ship, and grabbed his ankle just as he was going over.

Unfortunately my momentum combined with gravity took me over the side. I grabbed for the edge and was just barely able to hang on. We swung there for a moment. I held onto the ship with my left hand, the ankle of the cabin boy with my right and stared down at some very disappointed rocks. We were pulled back aboard. The boy looked stricken and would not leave my side.

My crew would not even meet my glance and all looked a bit ashamed of themselves. I decided not to go on about the incident or about the deliberate way in which they ignored my orders. They learned their lesson this day, it is one that will stand on its own.

We went to inspect the damage. Otter, the cabin boy I rescued, was still following along as though I were a mother duck. We lowered ourselves over the side of the ship at a much less lethal rate of speed and looked over the ship. It was just as the sound had indicated. The "back" of my poor ship was most surely broken. Her keel had been damaged by the impact. She was hurt, but thank God, still somewhat seaworthy.

We had made the temporary repairs that we could make and then pushed the ship from the rocks. We sailed safely around what I have now named Kjalarnes. Thorvald opposed me naming it this, but the name fit because it is where we damaged our keel. He put up less of a fight then he would have before the incident. He no longer had the backing of the crew in such matters, so without their moral support he just let it drop.

Our ship limped into a large inlet leading west, and it was here that we landed. We noticed there was wood for repairs and seemingly ample provisions so we could restock our supply of food.

We had been here for perhaps a day when one of my men found it. I was sitting in the shade and Otter was asking me all sorts of questions about my life. I felt a little uncomfortable with the attention, but he had been on the ship since the first trip and no one had really spoken to him. He seemed to be happy to have someone to talk to. One of my men ran up and said I had better come look at something. It was where they had been cutting down a tree for the repairs to the keel. In the dirt, by the tree, there were the tracks of perhaps seven or eight people, all barefoot.

At first I thought this might be a joke by Thorvald and some of the men, but upon further inspection it was obvious the tracks were not made by our men. Now I am in no way about to boast any sort of intimate knowledge of the feet of my men. This is the type of claim that would have me declared unfit for anything but playing about with women's hair and coordinating their outfits. These appeared too small and narrow to be the track of one of us. These were the footprints of what looked to be no more than adolescents.

Most of the men seemed to be trying to reconcile what Leif had told them against the evidence that was staring them in the face. Others gave up that line of thought and instead were trying to reconcile the tree they were chopping and what would be the most productive direction for it to fall. I didn't have anything to reconcile; I always felt the land had been inhabited, despite the fact I never saw the natives.

Thorvald made very little attempt at reconciling anything. He simply unsheathed his sword. He set his face in the manner of one who was trying to be very purposeful and he wanted others to be purposeful with him. Purpose washed over Rig and he stood by Thorvald and examined the footprints.

"They will have to go," said Thorvald very seriously and deliberately.

I looked up at David who seemed to be having a wonderful time doing lazy circles in the sky. I wondered if there was any way that I could join him. Obviously there wasn't. It looked as if I was going to have to stay on the ground and keep Thorvald from doing something very foolish.

I pulled Thorvald aside and explained to him the fact that not only were we unsure as to the nature of the natives, but that they seemed to be content to keep their distance from us. Furthermore, I explained to him how bad it would be to kill off a population that we may want to trade with in the future. Purpose never left his face. He slapped me on the back in a hard friendly way and made a grunt that meant he knew exactly what he was doing. I sighed in a way that was to convey to anyone who cared to be listening that I knew he knew what he was doing. It was just that I knew what he was doing was rather foolish and stupid.

Thorvald followed the tracks into the forest. He was closely followed by Rig and some of the other sailors who reckoned this would be more interesting than fixing the keel.

The group who was originally working on the tree, went back to work cutting it down, once they had figured out what direction would be best for it to fall.

I followed Thorvald's group. I concluded that perhaps one clear head in the bunch would do some good. Otter still, in a rather persistent manner, trailed after me.

We followed the tracks for about an hour. It was a clear trail. Whoever owned the footprints had obviously not regarded us a danger for they made no effort to hide their movements...or else we were being led off deliberately. That nagging notion had been with me since the beginning. I looked up and saw David flying slightly ahead of us. This was a bit of a comfort to me. If there were danger, I was fairly certain that he would somehow react to it. I could take it as a warning and respond accordingly.

We reached a clearing where we spied a small band of men. They were sitting about, conversing in a strange language. One was trying to start a fire, while another was skinning a rabbit. They were slim, a good bit smaller than us and clad only with clothes about their waists. They were of copper colored skin and deep black hair. Their faces were broad and very ugly. They seemed to be carrying weapons of stone along with bows and arrows.

We came out of the forest into the clearing. They didn't seem alarmed by our presence.

They all stood motionless. We stood, silently looking at each other, as if we were each waiting for the other to start the conversation. This was of course not going to happen. I have never been in this situation before. Granted, I'm used to dealing with strange and incomprehensible races. Anyone who has been to England is. This was different though. This was a new breed of man. I did the only thing I could think of. I unsheathed my sword and slowly laid it upon the ground in front of me. I believed the best first move was to convince them we were not hostile. My first move should have been to convince Thorvald that we were not hostile. As soon as my sword hit the ground, he pulled his sword and start running at them. Rig did the same and followed his overzealous leader.

It is unknown to me why, but the sight of Rig charging with a drawn sword prompted an angry response from David. Rig got no more than ten steps into his charge when David, diving at full speed, hit him square in the chest. The force of the blow knocked Rig off his feet and quite a distance backwards. His talons had found their mark deep in Rig's body. Rig was left on the ground gasping for air and bleeding heavily. It is a strange irony that David may have saved Rig's life.

Thorvald continued his charge alone. He scattered the natives and they ran into the woods. As he began to give chase, we heard a familiar twang, and the sound of something cutting through the air. Thorvald stopped, and fell backwards. He had an arrow sticking out of his chest. Death took him before we even reached his body.

We quickly gathered up Thorvald's lifeless body and Rig's injured body and hurriedly made our way back to the ship. We posted guards and scrambled furiously to finish. I pray we can make our ship seaworthy before revenge becomes the crew's battlecry.

Chapter 16

"These pathetic Skraeling will not get away with murder!" Hring screamed to the heavens. We sat around the fire and listened as he ranted and raved about the death of Thorvald. Hring wasn't particularly close to Thorvald, but he was one who seemed to enjoy conflict.

"They killed him with an arrow, hidden in the safety of the bushes. Fearing his brave charge!"

He stalked around the campfire in a half crouch as he made this point. He would stick his finger in the face of anyone who happened to be close enough just to add weight to his points.

"These weaklings would not even give him the honor of single combat. He never even saw his killer!"

Hring spoke very slowly and deliberately, presumably to make sure no one had any doubt as to how large a crime this was. He faced the fire and raised his arms to the sky.

"Oh great Thor, give us the courage and strength to carry out justice for the wrongly slain!"

Hring fell to his knees as he called to Thor. Our fire lengthened his shadow and enhanced the effect.

Hring the Swede, so named because of his father's lineage, was an odd sort of fellow. First and foremost, his most distinguishing characteristic was his incredible lack of size. He was small of stature and slight of build. He equaled out these shortcomings with volume. He was a very loud man. He seemed to make a point of having his voice, in any circumstance, be heard above everyone else's. When we laughed in a group, his was the loudest laugh. When we shouted, his was the loudest yell, and when we mourned, he wailed as if he too would soon pass. He is also the first to tell you of his great courage. Observation tells me that he is courageous only when he is backed by large numbers.

I listened to his ranting, knowing his motive. He wanted to "lead" us on a holy vendetta to avenge Thorvald. I can't say that I disagree. It is true that Thorvald attacked and intended to fight. He was a man of courage and action. He was also a man who would only fight you if he could see you. Killing him by hiding in ambush and firing from the shadows was an unforgivably dishonorable thing to do. Regardless of how I felt though, I could not allow my men to seek revenge.

I addressed the crew. I focused more on those who still practice the pagan religion of odinn. Hring lost the attention and support of the Christians as soon as he invoked the name of Thor. I folded my arms in front of my chest and turned my head to look at Hring, who was still stalking around the fire. I silently stared at him. He had not yet stopped talking. I assumed he felt the weight of my stare. He looked over to me and locked his eyes upon mine. His voice started to become less booming and more hesitant. My eyes followed him as he walked the semi circle the crew had formed around the fire. My crew is for the most part, with the exception of when an Eiriksson is aboard, a very loyal and professional group. I am the captain. The only one who could have pulled rank on me is now dead. I stood to speak and they gave me their full attention. Hring with the loss of support reluctantly sat down and listened to what I had to say.

I uncrossed my arms. As I began to speak, I waved for them to come in a little closer. I folded my hands in front of me and leaned just a tiny bit into them.

"Friends, we are all angered by what has happened here today," I said in my most measured and calming tone.

"He was a good man, and a good friend. Nothing would bring me more pleasure than avenging his death. But friends let us use our heads before following our emotions. These are an unknown people, in unknown numbers, living in unknown places. We are in no position to force an engagement. If we do, we may all share brave Thorvald's fate. Let us bide our time. When we return, let it be with force of numbers and take away their advantage."

I made sure that my speech was brief, logical and to the point. I avoided the emotional screaming, yelling and invocations to God. I would hope that most of my crew was above that.

"In the morning, we will finish the repairs to our ship, by midday we will leave this place behind. If anyone has anything they wish to say, they may speak freely."

I stood back and waited. No one made a move to speak, so I continued.

"Then we are agreed, we leave tomorrow with no further bloodshed and let justice come another day."

I wasn't looking for resounding cheers, which was good because I didn't get any. What I did get was most of my crew shaking their heads in affirmation. This was all I had expected out of them. I believe I can trust them to obey my wishes.

For the past several weeks of the journey, our morning had started the same way. First there would be a blood-curdling scream followed by a string of obscenities. The scream and the rude language were both products of Rig's mouth. These reactions are not the product of some nightmares or even of the previous night's stew. His tormentor, and the object of his ensuing verbal onslaught, is my falcon, David.

It seems that David's obsession with Rig has intensified. I have not been able to figure out what the connection is. At first it was just surprise assaults from the air. Who knows, perhaps something in Rig's hat looked edible to David. Now though, things seem to have escalated. David has gotten in the habit of perching very close to Rig as he sleeps. At first Rig found this to be annoying, but tolerable. As time went on, his reaction became more dramatic. Nowadays you can hear him in the mornings, falling over things as he backs away and screaming, "What do you want from me?" In fact, it is this reaction that usually wakes the camp up on time. Also, on this morning, it was the lack of this reaction that kept us from getting up on time.

David was perched near me when I awoke. I sat up and looked out to the horizon. The sun was higher in the sky than usual. I don't like waking up late. It is bad for my reputation to be the last man awake. I splashed water onto my face and wondered why I didn't hear the scream this morning. I looked over at David who seemed to be a little down. Or perhaps, a better word would be disappointed. It took a second to hit me, which considering that I am at my worst in the mornings anyway, was a record. But, I deduced, if the scream didn't wake me, then there must not have been a scream. I hardly thought that David took the morning off, considering the depth of his fixation with Rig. Therefore, Rig must not have been in his bed-roll when David got there.

I threw on my clothes as fast as I could, and moved quickly off the ship and on to the beach where work was being completed on our keel. I stopped one of the men as he was hauling fresh water to the ship.

"Have you seen Rig this morning?" I asked. I tried to be non-chalant about it, but the fact that I was hopping on one foot while still trying to pull the boot onto the other probably destroyed that facade.

"He went out with Hring and Hanson a few hours ago. They said they were hunting." He balanced the heavy pails on either side of the yoke he had across his shoulders.

"Did you see which way they went?" I said as I now went on to buckle my belt.

He sighed a little and fidgeted a bit under the yoke as he tried to point and balance the water at the same time. I got tired of his fidgeting. And since I wasn't maintaining my nonchalance very well anyway, I pushed the yoke of his back and let the water spill over the sand.

"Now," I said in a calm voice, and fully dressed body, "Can you show me which way they went?"

He glanced at the spilled water and looked at me as if I had just tossed him a lemming. He pointed to the spot where he had seen them enter the forest. I grabbed the young man firmly by both arms.

"Go arm yourself and bring some of the men. Meet me back here in two minutes. Go!" I slapped him on the back as he ran off.

I turned to go back to the ship to get my own weapons, when Otter appeared from behind me. He had my sword, shield, and helmet. I put on my arms as the other men joined me. I thanked Otter, mussed his hair and led my small band into the woods.

We followed the trail left by our shipmates. This wasn't difficult seeing as they made no attempt whatsoever to conceal their movements. We had been in the woods for the better part of an hour when we heard it. Screams, dreadful hideous screams. Our pace quickened as we made our way to the origin of the sound. It was there that I saw a nightmare unfold.

Our missing men had captured one of the natives and tied him between two trees. Hanson was leaning over a bush throwing up his breakfast as Hring laughed at him. The Skraeling they had tied appeared to be no more than a boy, and was wailing and pleading in his strange tongue. Fate had not yet allowed him to lose consciousness. He was awake and alert for the whole ordeal. They had made one straight deep cup down the length of his back, and then pulled the skin and muscle away.

Rig had his arms, elbow deep, in the boy's body. I could hear the wounded child crying as the blood poured from his wounds. I recognize what they were trying to do. Rig had his foot braced against the Skraeling's back and was pulling with all his might. He pulled and shook as he tried to dislodge the lungs from the boys living body. They were performing the blood eagle. Rig's intention was to pull the lungs out from the cut and spread them across the wretch's back.

I drew my sword and rushed out of the brush at them. Rig turned to me as my blade whistled past his face. I cleaved the head of the native in two. It was the fastest and most painless way I could think of to end his suffering. I looked at Rig for a moment. My sword was still embedded in the boy's head; Rig had not pulled his arms from the body of the Skraeling. I looked at him and then pulled my sword from the boy, striking Rig hard in the forehead with its pommel. He fell backwards, unconscious.

Hring rushed towards me. Spinning around, I struck him in the nose with my fist. The iron plating on the back of my glove crushed his nose flat. He lay on the ground crying like a woman. Hanson was still getting sick in the bushes. It was my belief that Hanson was nothing more than a dupe they had brought with them. I had him placed in irons along with his compatriots and taken back to the ship.

The work effort on the ship was doubled. There was a need to have the repairs done quickly. I didn't know if the natives had found the boy yet, but if they had, they may have come looking for revenge. I was not ready to risk the safety of my remaining crew on a fool's battle.

We completed the keel and were back at sea with astounding speed. Once away we turned our attention to our three vigilantes.

They were still in irons, and standing in a straight line. Rig wore a bump on his head the size of an egg. Hring was still bleeding from his smashed nose and Hanson, still sick from the sight of the tortured Skraeling, and could keep not even water in his stomach. I had a chair set several paces in front of them. Sitting down, I leaned back a little and put my feet up on a small stool.

"You have disobeyed my orders and in the process endangered the crew."

I picked at some lint on my sleeve as I spoke to them. I was trying very hard to give the impression that they meant very little to me.

"This is an act of mutiny and my way is clear."

I waved to some of the other men to come over. They drew their swords and put the tips at the throats of the three men. I continued to act as if this were any other order, such as raise the sail or let out the oars. I wanted those three miscreants to know that having them killed was going to mean as much to me as swatting a fly.

I looked at those I had chosen to carry out my wishes.

"On my word you will run these three through and dump their bodies in the ocean."

I removed a little piece of dried fish out of a pouch and fed it to David as the men readied themselves to carry out the punishment. Hring began to tear up and sniffle. Rig visibly turned white. Hanson just closed his eyes and prayed silently. At least, I thought he was praying. I could see his lips moving. I continued to let them wait for the order. I wanted the fear of death to sink in. Rig was shaking visibly and threw up on the deck. I got up from my chair and began to walk away.

"Pray the order never comes." I said as I walked to the prow.

They spent the rest of the trip home in irons, and were released when we reached Greenland. Gathering my things, I went to leave the ship. I would walk off this ship, and hopefully never return as captain. I'm not interested in the responsibility of leadership, and for now my thirst for adventure and discovery is gone. I passed Otter as I went to the gangplank. He was sitting in a coil of rope just staring out into the city.

"Where are your parents, boy?" I asked this knowing full well that they were not here. He answered with a non-committal shrug of his shoulders.

"I am staying here awhile. If you like, you may stay with me." I then walked down the plank.

I heard his footsteps right on my heels and soon he was by my side. I have secured temporary lodging for us. Tomorrow, I intend to take the money I have saved and buy Rik's place if I can. If not, I'm sure I can afford another farm. It will be good not to be working it alone.

Chapter 17

I have lived yet another profound day.

As I awoke that morning, I felt the weight of my years settling on me and holding my body down like an anchor. It was either that or last night's culinary experiment with herring. Considering the taste that lingered in my mouth, I am going to blame it on the herring.

I stretched and rose from my bed. I listened to the symphony of cracks and creeks emanating from various points of my body. After a couple times around the room, the orchestra rested and I moved in relative silence again, except for the gurgling sounds in my stomach doing their best to play an unaccompanied encore.

As I completed my last circle, I looked out my bedroom window and saw Otter practicing with the sword I had bought him. His clumsy movements look all too familiar. Sometimes it doesn't seem like all that long ago that I was standing in his place. I watched Otter as he swung the blade around his body. The heavy weapon's momentum kept him moving, even when he didn't want to. He wound up spinning off balance and falling into the dirt. That was me so many years ago.

I poured a bowl of water from the brass pitcher on my nightstand and splashed the water onto my face. As I stood hunched over the bowl, the cool liquid dripped off on its own power. I didn't move from that place until the morning air had completely dried my face. This gave me time to debate as to whether I really wanted to be out of bed. The more I thought about it, the better going back to bed sounded. I eventually decided that it would be a good character builder to resist the sin of sloth and face the day. I grabbed the pitcher and raised it to God in celebration of my will power and poured the water into my mouth. Some of the water splashed off the dents in the pitcher spout and into my eyes. This served to wake me even further. The liquid washed over the back of my tongue, taking away the acrid, lingering taste of last night's dinner. Fully awake, I replaced the pitcher and went to dress.

I picked up a shirt from one of the many that littered my bedroom floor. If my mother saw this mess she would tug my ear so hard my lobe would hang to my knees. I have always been a bit on the messy side, and I like to use the excuse that I am too old to change. Under the shirt, was another one of those letters. I picked it up and turned it over a few times in my hands. It was made of heavy brown paper, like the others, and bore the same ornate dragon head seal of Leif Eiriksson. The sound I made when I tossed it over my shoulder was a sort of a snorting laugh. I didn't even bother to open this one. Leif should really stop wasting paper on these messages.

Over the past few years he has sent me dozens of messages asking me to work with his colonization efforts. It has been five years since our return from Vinland. To date I have rejected all offers to go back and help. This seemed like a better place to raise a child. Otter has grown into a fine young man. He has become a very popular person around Hvarf. Known for his wine red hair, extreme intelligence, and excellent manners.

I took Otter in basically because I felt sorry for him. In the larger scheme of things, it was my way of repaying Rik for what he had done for me. I had no idea what I was bringing in though. I was ready to take care of someone who was like me as a child. This was not the case. Otter was far smarter and more mature than I was at his age. Hell, he may be far smarter and mature than I am at age 32, who knows? He will not speak of his family, but I can only assume they were a well-educated lot. There were nights when I would go to his bedroom while he was sleeping to put an extra blanket over him and I would hear him talking in his sleep, in Latin. He also spoke French and English.

It was a pleasant surprise to find that he had been raised as a Christian. I would not have to go through the long process of converting him from a senseless pagan religion. It also gave him a moral base that my upbringing lacked. I would never have to worry about him taking covert trips to Madam Grunnhilde's. With his looks, though, I doubt he would ever need her establishment. He also seemed to have no attraction to mead. One less headache that I, and he, would have to deal with. My only worry is his outgoing nature. He seems to trust nearly everyone. Considering the Christian hating factions among our people, this is a trait that could get him killed. His friends all seem to be of good character, but I still worry when he comes home late. One just never knows.

I called for Otter to get on the roof and start the repairs. He picked himself up off the ground and headed toward the ladder. I planned to join him when I was finished dressing. Winter had been unusually hard and it would take some extra work this spring to keep the house in shape.

I managed to purchase Rik's old house. I probably paid more for it than I should have. Technically I should not have paid for it at all. The house was never actually sold. As his sole heir, I should have had exclusive rights to it. Considering that I had also not been back to the house in well over a decade, and that I may still be the one blamed for Rik's murder, in the name of peace, I gave the family who was squatting in it, the home's fair value. To their credit, they did keep it up well. It was worth the money to have my home back. It was a good way to put the fruits of years at sea to use and it provided a permanent shrine for Rik's memory and the shield he gave me so many years ago.

My first task after buying Rik's hall was to erect a rune stone in his memory. There was a large boulder at the eastern border of my land. Upon it I carved the likeness of a falcon. Its wings spread out to the east and west. For hours, I labored with my chisel to create a tribute to the man who had become my friend, mentor, and second father. Within the very feathers of the bird, I carved the words that would sum up the life of the one who had raised me. I wrote of how he saved me from the jaws of the wolves. My conversion to Christianity and salvation from Hell was credited to Rik. Even the moments when we rode through the fields, laughing and playing in mock combat were carved eternally into stone. With every thought and every feeling the wings of the falcon became wider. My last carving was that of the Christian cross over the head of the falcon. It was all I had room for. The rest of the stone was covered with runes. I mounted my horse and rode away. I originally intended to drag it back, closer to the house. Upon reflection, it is far better left where it is. This stone is the first thing visitors to my land will see and the last thing I will see when I leave.

At first I was a bit uneasy about living here. I felt I could never get over the memory of Rik's horrible death and my uneasiness about why he had been killed. I couldn't sleep our first few nights here. When I finally did manage to let go of my consciousness, nightmares would follow. Every evening I was brought back to that same place, that grove of trees where I hid as a child and watched the silhouettes of evil men as they stripped and tore at the one thing that gave meaning to my childhood.

One night, I didn't wait for the dreams to bring me to that place. I took my bedroll and placed it on the spot where Rik had taken his final breath. Lying on the ground, I could feel the grass under my hand. My fingers dug into the soil. I sat up and inspected this handful of dirt. It was no different than any other dirt I had encountered in my life. In fact it was probably several grades better than any dirt anywhere in England. That realization alone had to be worth something. How could a small plot of simple dirt hold any terror for me? I flattened my hand and blew the soil into the night air. The breeze carried it away. Sleep came a little easier that night. The bad dreams still come occasionally, but at least there now seems to be a balance.

I also remember being a youth here. I was happy. I wanted to give Otter that same happiness. So we stayed. After time, I learned not only to live with my demons, but I also realized that Rik had a pretty good time with an adopted son around.

I got outside and thanked God for a day that did not leave me longing to swim in a lake of fire. Winter had been that hard this year.

We finally had a beautiful, warm spring day. I was actually looking forward to a day of work outside.

I made my way up the ladder. Each rung gave a little as put my weight on it. Apparently the roof is not the only thing that needs fixing. Otter was already pounding away. I carefully negotiated the sloping roof, looking for holes and weak spots.

From the top of the roof I could see, far off in the distance, riders heading our way. We didn't get too many visitors up here, outside of Otter's friends and occasionally parents of daughters who thought Otter would make a perfect husband. I told Otter to keep working and I went down to wait for our visitors. They arrived soon afterwards. Two men rode up the road to our house. They were impeccably dressed in high leather boots and the clean black uniforms of those who serve Leif Eiriksson.

"Greetings," I said to them as they brought their horses to a full stop.

David swooped down and landed on my head, curious about the visitors.

"We bring you greetings from Leif Eiriksson," they said in a way that was proper and rehearsed. I began to wonder if Leif actually taught them to speak in unison like that or if they had just done this many, many times.

The older of the two bent over a little and petted the neck of his brown horse. Large muscles in the horse's shoulder began to twitch as he did this. I could not tell the color of the man's hair, because of his coned helmet and chainmail which hung down from it and fell over his shoulders, but the lines extending from the edge of blue eyes exposed him as no younger than myself.

"Lord Eiriksson has dispatched us to extend an invitation for you to meet with him in his hall," he said in a very proper and rehearsed way.

He continued to pet the horse as his partner, who had delivered what was apparently his only line, stared off majestically into the distance, content with a job well done. His older partner sat straight up in his saddle again.

123

"We are not to return without you."

This was said in a very proper, scripted and mildly threatening way. I'm pretty sure the messenger spent many hours practicing how to be threatening in a proper and scripted way. Not being one for an argument (especially one I would lose) I informed Otter that I would be back by nightfall.

Otter stood up. He seemed uneasy. And why not? Seeing his adoptive father taken under armed escort was not an everyday occurrence. I smiled and told him his allowance depended on the roof being done by my return. He assured me that it would be done, and went back to pounding. He gave me a nervous smile as I mounted my horse. I wanted to do something, anything to make him feel better about my leaving. I hate the idea of Otter sitting on the roof worrying about me. If Rik had given me that type of opportunity, I would have been in disguise and beating down the door of Madam Grunnhildes so fast it would make their heads spin. That was me though, Otter is quite different.

My escorts and I rode together silently. They had completed their mission and apparently run the gambit of their script, so they had very little left to say. My horse, though a beautiful deep black stallion, was no great conversationalist. His smooth gate combined with the stimulating nature of my companions had me nearly asleep by the time we reached Eirik's hall.

Eirik's hall, named for Leif's late father, had one outstanding attribute. It was not its general biggness, because as far as big things go it was definitely at the top of the list. Nor was it the riches that adorned it. Not that those features were unimpressive, although the emerald studded mosaic of a school of herring was a little overdone. What caught my eye the most was the extreme whiteness. Everything was a clean, rich white. His furniture was made of sea ivory and white marble. Silken, cream colored drapes hung from the entryways and rugs made of white bear covered the floors. I looked at myself and the state I was in after fixing the roof and the long ride. I felt filthy. I was afraid to touch anything. Knowing Leif, that was the point. He wanted those who entered his domain to feel like the unwashed. As far as status stunting tricks go, this was a good one. I felt not good enough to be in his presence. It is a trick I shall remember.

They brought me to a room where Leif was seated at the head of a long white table. Leif seemed not at all the worse for wear. He was dressed in red robes that denoted his position of leadership with a coat of light mail underneath. He did not rise. He just motioned with his hand for the messengers to leave us and then spread the same hand out in invitation to one of the chairs by him. There was food already on my plate. We were lunching on cuts of beef and vegetable broth.

"Thank you for coming," he said as he cut his meat.

He never raised his eyes to meet mine. He just spoke—as if to the air. I started to eat my soup. I was not going to ask him what he wanted. He went to all that trouble to get me there, he could get around to telling me what he wanted without any prompting. He sat straight in his chair and began eating. He addressed the air again.

"I want you to return to Vinland and take over leadership of the colonies," he said.

This was a funny thing for Leif to say to the air. It didn't seem incredibly interested in answering. I sat there and ate my soup; the air was not about to give its opinions of Vinland policy and I would not answer until spoken to directly. He noted my silence and probably assumed it meant that I declined.

He looked to his right and clapped his hands once. A servant came out with a large bag. It was obviously quite heavy by the way he was struggling. If his raisin like appearance was any indication, the servant was quite advanced in years. His load was apparently a weighty one and he was doing everything in his power to make sure we knew just how much effort he had put forth to bring it to us.

His wheezing was like an off key whale song. He dropped the load on the floor and dragged it the rest of the way. He then panted heavily and set it by my chair. After he had straightened up and put his hand on his back to indicate the pain the bag had induced, he took a few more deep breaths. Once his breath was caught, with Godlike effort, he opened the bag.

It was filled with gold pieces. I could not see how the air would possibly have any use for gold. Leif stopped eating and for the first time looked at me directly.

"What is your answer?" He asked.

He sat there waiting for my response. This time he made more than a little eye contact. In fact, in the moments he awaited my answer I am not even sure that he blinked. I looked at the gold and thought of all the things it would be good for. I also thought of Otter and how happy he seemed here and how normal and peaceful my life had become. Regardless of the value of that bag, and it was considerable, I rejected the offer.

"I'm sorry," I said as I wiped my mouth on a cloth, taking great care to leave a stain. I pushed myself away from the table, "I'm just not interested."

Leif calmly resumed eating and began to speak to the air again.

"I do have something else to offer you." He said in a tone not unlike that of a horse salesman.

"There was a man named Rik who was murdered here several years ago. Many blamed his young adopted son for the killing."

My skin flared. As far as I knew I was still wanted for that crime.

"The truth of course was quite different. Rik wasn't just murdered...his death was an execution, sanctioned from very high above you and I."

He shifted his attention from the meat and began to eat his soup as he passed on this information. I felt numb. Leif had just taken my brain from east to west. I was no longer blamed for Rik's death. But, then who was? Who would have ordered Rik's execution? And why?

"I will promise you this...neither my father or any part of my family had anything whatsoever to do with Rik's death." Leif said in anticipated defense.

Nothing could have been farther from my mind. I never knew Rik to bear any ill will toward Eirik the Red, or any of his family. Also, if he wanted a man dead, Erik was not the type for backhanded tricks. He would stand right in front of him, smiling, while his soldiers publicly cut the man to shreds. He put his utensils down and stood up. Planting both hands upon the table, Leif leaned toward me.

"The story on public record is that Rik was a traitor, an enemy of the crown of Norway. He owned a ship. It flew the colors of the Danes. This ship plundered the shores of Norway for years before she was eventually sunk off the coast of Greenland. My father was asked to bring Rik to justice. Considering some past debt that he owed Rik, he allowed him to live in peace, and enjoy the fruits of his plunder. My father and Rik are now gone. I owe nothing to this man or his family. His dishonor will follow his children and his children's children for generations. By the way, that cabin boy you adopted...how is he fairing?"

Leif never once mentioned that I had any connection to Rik, but his veiled threat was easily read. I could live with the ramifications that were sure to come but I was not going to have Otter inherit these problems. I picked up one of the silver chalices and took a drink of wine. I would have liked to answer him but my throat had suddenly gone dry. I could not accept that Rik was perceived as a traitor or in favor with the Danes.

"To be as plain as I can be," Leif said as he backed away from the table and bent down to pick up the money bag, "if you do this for me, only long enough to get the colony under control, this gold is yours, and the records will be corrected to clear Rik's name of any wrongdoing."

I didn't see where I had a choice. It was obvious that if I didn't do this there were harsh penalties to pay. If I did, I would clear my father's name and become rather wealthy. There was only one other factor that I wanted to deal with. My voice found itself as soon as I thought of it.

"Leif, I have one question before I accept your most....generous offer. If that man's son didn't do it, and the Rik person's death was ordered, do you know who put forth the command?"

He half-smiled.

"I don't know who did, but it is said that Rik's falcon, who resembles the falcon that travels with you, did not leave the man without injury. If you find a man with the scars of a falcon's claw, you have found your killer."

He turned to leave. I guess my audience was over. He spoke as he walked away.

"Your ship is waiting in the harbor and I have a pool of men you can draw from as a crew."

I picked up the gold and began to make my way for the door. Leif stopped and looked over his shoulder at me.

"Harald, if you find this killer and he should, say, have an accident. Blame it on the natives of Vinland and I will see the law looks into it no further."

With that, he walked off and disappeared into another room.

That last statement told me he knows Rik's death is meaningful to me, he knows who did it, he knows the killer is in Vinland, he knows the real reason why Rik was killed and he also knew it was better not to give me the name. I don't mind—he has given me enough information to eventually find this man.

Our journey was to take place nearly immediately. I explained the situation to Otter and told him he could stay here. I would leave him half the bag of gold and the house was his until my return. He was the first in line next day to sign on for the crew. Bless his heart.

I was very selective in forming my crew. I chose those with nautical skills as well as good military skills. Another prerequisite was they had to be of Christian faith. By the time the selection process was over I had, not a crew, but a professional army of Christian fighting men. We set sail this very day with a strong west wind.

Chapter 18

God had apparently heard my prayers, for our voyage was without incident. Well almost without incident. On one of our three ships, the Raven, there was a small dispute over the rowing duties. This dispute quickly erupted into a major disagreement, and then a full-scale fight. After a few minutes of warring, the other soldiers subdued the combatants. To me this was not necessarily a bad thing, it just shows me my men have spirit. Even so, once we get to the mainland, I will have to keep the combatants in separate patrols. If we find ourselves in a fighting situation, I wouldn't want them to take advantage of the confusion of battle and kill their own compatriot.

The time it took to get to our destination gave me the opportunity to completely study and prepare my men for what would be faced in Vinland. I spent most of my time with the maps and writings from the scribes that Leif had provided for me. I made a point of committing every detail of the maps to memory. If this turns into a military campaign, I prefer not to provide knowledge of the lay of the land as a weapon for the enemy.

I was locked away in my cabin, face buried in a map when I heard the call.

"Land HO!!" came a bellow from the deck.

It took us barely two weeks and we were looking over the coast of Vinland. The blanket of night hid all but the faintest signs of land. Light from over a dozen small fires dotted the black sky. It was like fireflies caught in tar. This land has sure changed from the last time I was here. It is a strange feeling to see it as a colony now, when I remember it as only wild territory. Ever since Leif had returned from Vinland, he had busied himself with the task of selling land to anyone he could and then shuttled them over from Greenland.

I'm certain in order to make a sale, Leif led these people to believe that the land was rich and fertile. I'm certain he would tell them that the land flowed with mead and blondes if he thought it would get someone to buy. Sometimes I get the feeling Leif is better suited for selling used horses than for governing Greenland.

There was a large fire on top of a small hill. More than likely, there was some sort of gathering going on up there. They had probably established a Vinland Thing. That was to my advantage, I could address the colonists as one instead of having them wake up to the sight of military occupation.

Vinland had three major problems that needed immediate attention. First, the number of men far exceeded the number of available women in the colony. This resulted in an unusual number of violent incidents between jealous husbands and opportunistic lovers. There was also an unusual number of men going into the business of sheep herding, but there isn't anything I can do about that.

Next there was the problem of the natives. Our first contact with them has not been forgotten or forgiven. Ever since they put down stakes, the colonists have been subject to a relentless series of harassing raids. No military effort has managed to solve the problem and retaliation has only aggravated the situation.

Last and not least is the problem of the clashing religions. Christians are constantly at risk of the intolerance of the pagans. There have been instances of sacrifices of natives and Christians to odinn by zealous pagans. I found this to be a particularly repulsive crime. The worshipers of odinn will just have to excuse me for my biases. This situation will not continue.

We docked the boat in a dark cove and disembarked as silently as possible. Alone, I walked up the hill to the bonfire. There was a meeting of sorts going on. It looked like I had caught them at their Thing. There were several men huddled around the bonfire. The group had polarized into two sides. As I took a good look into the crowds, I saw firelight reflecting off their weapons. It appeared that every man was armed. This was not unexpected. I watched from the bushes. I have heard an infestation of rodents is one of the problems with this colony. I sat back and listened to one of the rat's speak.

"You Christians are the problem. Odinn is mad at us for allowing you onto this new land. You have made the land sick, and you must be gone before it will ever heal."

I remembered the speaker; it was Hring, one of my ex-crewmembers. Apparently, he learned nothing from the lesson of mercy I tried to teach him. The grumbling in the crowd told me that not everyone shared Hring's rather narrow view on the subject. In fact, the audience reaction seemed to be half-and-half. My ears perked to the rustle of leaves and clanking of steel coming up from behind me. My men had found their places. It was now time for me to go interrupt this meeting.

I fastened my cape and walked into the crowd. I was a stranger in their colony, and they parted as I passed through. I walked up behind Hring and tapped him on the shoulder. He turned to face me and looked me square in the chest plate of my armor. He looked up into my face and let out a little "eep" sound. He apparently recognized me. His hand went to his now crooked nose and looked deeply into my eyes.

"Sit down!" I said in a low course voice.

He got the message and went off into the crowd. I motioned for everyone to sit down. They milled about for a moment. Apparently confused as to what to do. Some sat, many crossed their arms and just stared, some just wandered about the crowd muttering questions to their comrades. They didn't know me.

I rested my hand on the hilt of my sword. The armor I was wearing was quite weighty and uncomfortable. I was beginning to itch in places that would damage what little credibility I had with these people if I scratched. I may have been in discomfort, but my appearance was probably the only thing that gave these folks pause, and me, their attention. I was in heavy mail with some plate armor on my shoulders and chest. My long black cape was fastened by a golden broach, and my conical helmet completed my protection. I will say this…I looked impressive. It was obvious to everyone that I had not come to preach a sermon. I removed my helmet and spoke to the crowd.

"Our leader, Leif Eiriksson, is not pleased at the lawlessness and the lack of progress of this colony. He has sent me to fix the problem. From this day forward, I am the law. You will live and die on my word and my word alone."

The muttering raised its volume at this point. I waited for it to die down before continuing.

"I am also dissolving all Thing activities. Self rule does not work here. From now on, you will be ruled."

Those who were sitting got to their feet. The muttering became shouts and centered around sentiments like "the Thing is a fundamental right of the people" and "you can't take this right away." No matter to me—they had to know I meant business.

They were angry, shouting, cursing, but maintained their distance. I spoke on Leif's authority. They feared me as they would him. It took longer for the complaining to die down this time. I waited patiently then continued my address.

"As of today there will be no more sacrifices to any God, period. Whether that sacrifice be animal or human. I am in no way saying that you may not worship your own God, but I am putting an end to the violent rituals whether they be Christian or to odinn. Also, there will be no more hunting and killing of the Skraelings. We will react defensively only and attempt to openly trade with them."

Hring jumped up. He was surrounded by his supporters. I was not surprised to see an ugly hat in the background of Hring's friends. Someone had to be pulling his strings.

"You will not tell us how to worship," he said as he spit on the ground and took three steps toward me.

I put my hands behind my back and smiled, just a little, at him. This seemed to make him even angrier.

"You know your rules don't affect the Christians, those weaklings don't sacrifice so you have made a law that affects only us."

He was nearly foaming at the mouth as he said this. Apparently I had touched a nerve. Judging by his reaction I had touched it with something rather heavy and painful.

"I don't believe I opened the floor to questions or comments," my steady moderate tone seemed to increase his rage.

He drew his sword; ten of his friends joined him as he did this. Rig hung back and just watched.

"You are a dead man. Leif is not here with you. By what power do you hope to impose your will?"

I raised my arm and David came down from the sky and settled on my wrist. Rig not only hung back at the sight of David, but he disappeared altogether. At this signal, over one hundred soldiers came out of the forest. They were in full armor and had their weapons drawn. They formed a semicircle behind me. David flew off into the sky again. I drew my sword and pointed it at Hring's throat.

"Any other questions?"

Of course nobody answered. They quietly dispersed back to their homes. I realize this mission will require me to reach deeply in my soul for strength and stamina—but I also know there is no greater purpose than to avenge Rik's murder and preserve his legacy.

Chapter 19

The weeks have moved slowly. Each day brings new challenges. The only thing I can compare this to is the herding of sheep. Sheep are not exceptionally bright animals, and they have this uncanny knack of getting themselves into the most unlikely sort of trouble. And they are easy prey for even the most inept predator. For all intents and purposes, that is my colony.

After forty-nine days of martial law, the sheep seem to be coming into line. We no longer have the violent and bloody conflicts that used to arise over the women in the colony. Of course, when I arrived I also brought with me over a hundred soldiers. This insured that if any of these conflicts were to arise, I would most certainly win.

Once Otter arrived in the colony, many of the women lost interest in anyone else who was here. Needless to say, there was a boom in the popularity of sheep herding. Persecution of Christians within the colony seems to have stopped altogether, but some of the worshipers of odinn are still capturing and sacrificing members of the native population. This is doing absolutely nothing to enhance our relations with them. Despite our best efforts, we cannot stop their sudden attacks. It would be a different story if they would come out of the woods for a straight fight, but they never do. Somebody is suddenly hit with an arrow and when we race into the forest to find the assailant, there is no one there. This situation also makes it incredibly difficult to open up any sort of trade with them.

I returned to my newly built home after examining the site of yet another sacrifice. The blood eagle had been spread over another Skraeling. I closed my eyes and tried to forget what I had just seen. The vision of the young native's face...twisted...contorted with pain,

135

formed into a macabre death mask, will haunt me for the next several hours. Whoever did this one was far less sloppy than when I witnessed Rig and Hring do it. The idea that someone actually has done this enough times to get good at it disturbs me on a number of levels.

I opened the door to my log home. I missed my hall back in Greenland. This one was drafty and less than a quarter the size. There were only two rooms at the moment, a large main room and a bedroom. There would, of course, be improvements to make over the course of time, but for now I don't like it.

Otter had gone riding with yet another one of the colony's women. Regardless of the shortage of females, he is never short of feminine attention. Of course for Otter that is normal.

Another relationship back to normal is that of Rig and David. Morning screams had once again become the norm. This was starting to take its toll on Rig though. It became obvious that he was no longer sleeping. He had also fallen into the habit of talking to himself. I can still find no logical reason for David's behavior, but that doesn't discount the fact that it is actually quite entertaining.

I remember well the words of Leif, and have been on the lookout for anyone with scars that resemble something a falcon would leave. Rig is the only one who fits that description. He has David's mark imbedded on his chest, but I was there when that happened so he is out of the running. I was thinking of having every man strip for an inspection, but not only is that an irrational order that I believe the people would not tolerate, but it is also an order that will give the colonists the idea that the shortage of women is beginning to get to me. As a leader, I do not wish to reflect that sort of image.

I went to lie on my bed to catch a few hours rest before the night's activity. I have decided to stop these sacrifices once and for all. This is Mayday, the spring celebration to odinn; this would be a prime time to sacrifice. When the pagans make their offerings to odinn, I will be there.

I drifted into a fitful sleep. In my dreams, the victims of past sacrifices surround me. They look at me with their death masks and mouth words I can't understand. Maggots feed at their festering wounds, as they agonize, praying in their strange tongue for release. In my mind they are forever tortured...undying. I was awakened by one of my soldiers shaking me furiously. I had overslept.

"Sir, three men passed our seventh check point, we followed them as they captured three of the Skraeling. They have brought them to the north clearing. Your standing orders were to follow and observe but not to act until you were there."

I put my hand on the young man's shoulder as I rose from my bed. I followed him on foot into the forest. We arrived at the North clearing to watch as a small band of men from the colony prepared to hang the natives.

They had bent some of the pine trees so that their tops were near to the ground. These were secured with ropes to ensure the tree-top would stay at about shoulder level. Then the Skraelings were tied with one end of a rope around the throat and the other to the treetop.

I looked over the small group and saw that Hring was their leader. I had suspected this from the beginning but had no proof. I had thirty of my soldiers circle the clearing, behind the cover of brush while Hring sang his invocation to the gods. He was out of tune. That seemed predictable. We moved out of the brush and into the clearing at a dead run. On first sight of us, they cut the ropes securing the trees. Treetops sprung into the air like a catapult, taking their helpless victims with them. When the trees sprung back to their natural straight up position the momentum generated threw the men forward, the ropes around their necks stopped them suddenly. There was a sickening crack as their necks broke. The limp bodies swung from the trees.

Hring and his friends tried to run but found themselves surrounded. They were beaten with the pommels of the swords of my soldiers. My orders had been to capture, not kill. I had plans and needed them alive. One of the men approached me.

"Sir, shall we cut the Skraeling down from the trees?" He asked, a bit flushed from the night's excitement.

"No," I said as I gazed into the forest, "I need their bodies to remain there. Did we find where these men got their sacrifices?"

"No sir," he said in an attentive military fashion.

137

"Get them to tell you where the Skraeling village is, I will need to go there in the morning." I sheathed my sword and began to walk home, the soldier stopped me.

"What if they are...reluctant?" He smiled as he said this. We both knew what he was getting at.

Most of the people in the colony were angrier with those who were doing the sacrifices that caused the Skraeling raids than with the Skraeling's themselves. Granted, the Skraelings fought like cowards, but they were just retaliating to actions taken against them. These fighting men of mine have wanted to get their hands on those colonists who were responsible for the wounding and occasional death of their peaceful comrades for quite some time.

"Do what you need to do, just make sure come morning they are alive and we have directions to the village."

With that, I turned and left. My voice cracked a little as I gave the order. It was easily justified. Rig and his friends were getting what they deserved. I gave my men an order and by morning they would have the information I was looking for. I would not think about what they had to do to get what I wanted. I thought it would be that straight forward. It wasn't.

I listened to the screams of tortured men for the rest of the night. I tried putting my blanket over my face to muffle the sound. Their cries of anguish bled through the cotton and down, and were as audible as if I were there. My mind began to imagine what my soldiers were doing to them. Occasionally, I winced in phantom pains at the thought of some of the torturous devices they may have used. Sleep would not come, even after the screams disappeared into the crisp night air. I began to wonder if I could carry out what I had in store for those criminals.

Morning came and I went back to where the night's sacrifices took place. One of my men presented me with the directions I had asked for. Rig lay panting on the ground. At least, it appeared to be Rig. His face had been beaten to an unrecognizable pulp. The ground around him was soaked with blood. I couldn't bring myself to congratulate the men on a job well done.

I took a detail of men and some gifts of cloth and food for the savages. We departed very early in the morning. There was no trail; we just walked straight into the forest. Most of the morning was spent hacking our way through the dense forest. It took us forever to go a short distance. In some spots, the forest almost became like night. The canopy above choked off the sunlight. By midday, I began to think that our directions were useless. Of course this was a difficult call to make, distance was hard to judge when it took so long just to go a short way.

We came upon a clearing, just past midday. The sun was high and directly above us. By my calculations we had another half day of light left. After a short rest, I sent out five teams of two to search the woods around the clearing. After another quarter day, we still came up with absolutely nothing. We were preparing ourselves for the hike back when we heard a very audible sneeze. Each of our heads turned toward the sound. After a long moment of uncomfortable silence, we heard the sneeze again. This time it was accompanied by the sound of rustling leaves. Whoever had the vapors, was now running away.

We followed the trail of broken branches and footprints. Until, quite unexpectedly, we were standing in the middle of the Skraeling camp. It was nearly impossible to see unless you were in it. The cool veil of the leaves hid it almost completely from view. In a straight line, for someone who knew where he was going, it was less than a morning's walk from our colony. I felt very uncomfortable with the enemy living so close to us.

Upon our arrival, the Skraeling scattered and hid in their lodges. Their homes looked like turtle shells covered in skins, very primitive. This was by no means a race on our level. A small band of them appeared from the forest. They had painted faces and wore feathers in their long black hair. All of them had bows and arrows slung across their backs. They were clothed only with skins hanging about their waists. Some of my men reached for their swords; I immediately ordered them to stand down and not to touch their weapons.

In front of the group was the one who appeared to be the leader. I took the gifts from one of my men and slowly walked forward. He met me about half way and took the gifts from my arms. He examined them and seemed most pleased with the red cloth. He said something in his strange language and some of the women came and took the gifts from him. Clinging to one of the women was a young boy, no more than seven. He was obviously terrified. He also had a bad case of the sniffles. Apparently his sneezes were our beacon to the camp.

Neither of us spoke the other's language, so communication was difficult. I walked back to my men and motioned for the natives to follow us. We walked back into the forest. Very slowly and cautiously they followed us, always with bows drawn and arrows aimed. We eventually got to the clearing where last night's sacrifice took place. Hring and his four compatriots were bound and standing by the trees.

It appeared the Skraeling chief recognized them. He pointed and started speaking to his companions. I walked over to Hring, he began to beg and cry for his life. He pleaded with me not to hand him over to the savages. I promised him I wouldn't.

I motioned for the chief to come over to me. He and four of his warriors came. I pointed up to the trees where the bodies of three of his men hung. I could see the fury in him begin to rise. He could not take his eyes off them. Tears welled up in the eyes of his warriors as they looked upon the treatment of their people. I then pointed to the group of men we had caught and bound. Hring was still pleading with me. I reminded him of my promise. This seemed to comfort him.

I had been successful in conveying the idea that these were the people responsible for the murder of the chief's friends. There was a long pause. I then turned to the captain of my guard.

"The order is given." I said.

Hring cast a sudden look of abject horror as five of my men drew their swords and ran him and his pagan followers through. They were killed one by one, terror overtaking whoever was next in line. It seemed each scream was louder and more agonizing than the last. The already bloodstained ground soaked up the rest of the precious fluid and it poured from their deep wounds. They writhed on the ground for a while and died soon after. This seemed to satisfy the chief. He took one of the feathers out of his hair and gave it to me. I smiled back at him. Then turned to leave.

I walked, but I couldn't feel my feet. The world around me seemed to be going much slower. I tried to feel something, but I was dead inside. A persistent icy sensation in my stomach was all I could sense. Many times I have killed in self-defense, or during a battle. Never have I ordered the death of a man. They were helpless, beaten, much like when I first killed so long ago. Was the price of peace truly worth this sort of sacrifice?

Now, I will sleep…perhaps later this feeling, or lack of feeling, will dissipate. If I keep telling myself that, perhaps I will believe it and perhaps it will become true.

Chapter 20

It wasn't long there after that we began trading with the Skraeling. They didn't exactly consider us allies, but we were no longer the enemy. It seems the decision to discipline my men in a way for all to see was well received by them. Unfortunately the decision was less popular amongst the colonists.

Predictably, there was overwhelming support from the Christians among us. To them, this was just one more smiting that God had brought down upon the lawless. To the pagan believers, it was a slap in the face. They saw it as me favoring the life of a worthless savage over the life of one of my own. Despite the fact that the native raids have been done away with, they still will not accept that I did what was right. Even so though, they along with the Christians benefited from the trading between the Skraeling and us.

These Skraeling have absolutely no sense when it comes to trade. They will trade three to four pelts for a swatch of red cloth barely big enough for me to blow my nose. They will give us fine leather goods and meat in trade for a tin of mead. They drink it here and go away with nothing. Where were these guys when I was buying my last horse? The one thing they prize above all is our weapons. They will do anything to get steel. I see this as a really bad idea. I have given an order that no one is to trade a weapon with these savages, but I'm sure that it is going on out of my line of vision.

I predict that someday there will be conflicts with these people and we will be fighting our own weapons. That is a worry for the future though. For the moment, it appears I have solved the problems that I had come here to solve.

Colony life seems to suit Otter. He has an adventurous spirit and an insatiable curiosity. In fact, the only thing the kid lacks is some a sense of humor, but I'm sure he will develop one someday.

Otter has recently been the recipient of a great legacy. David has found that his head makes a better roost than mine. I am not wholly opposed to this idea. A leader can hardly walk around with a bird on his head. Unfortunately for Otter, David is getting on in years and would rather ride than fly. Oh well, this is something that the boy is just going to have to get used to.

Over the past month, we have built the colony's first church. This was a major event for those of us who are of the Christian faith. Leif was pleased with the fact that things were back under control. As a gesture of good will, he sent us a priest named Ivar to teach in the church. We now get a proper service once a week.

I put the feather the Skraeling chief gave me in my hair and packed red cloth into my bag. I was invited to come and eat with the chief this day. At least I thought I was invited. We still are not even close to verbal communication, so we speak in pictures and hand signs. I was either going to his village for lunch or I had misinter-preted his meaning and I would be going off to wed his daughter. Lunch was my preference.

I walked to the village. The chief and his family welcomed me. I presented him with the cloth. This brought squeals of delight from his wife and at least a smile from him. They in return gave me a cape made out of the hide of brown bear. I tried to explain that the cloth was a gift, but they had none of it and didn't seem happy until I put the cape on. After which, they smiled and laughed and slapped me on the back. I seem to have become quite popular with them. I think they see me as their friend for vindicating those who had been mur-dered. I can't say I don't enjoy their company. At this point I would stay in Vinland, if for no other reason, to study the natives.

We had a lunch of deer meat, and a soup I couldn't identify. I have learned that if you are going to eat with these people it is in your best interests not to look at what you are eating. For all you know it may be looking back at you.

After dinner we smoked the pipe. I have no idea what they burn in that thing, but after about three puffs, I see the naked English women again. That is a good thing. I missed them.

I spent the afternoon and early evening in his tent. We conversed as best we could. If we are to stay, eventually someone is going to have to learn their language. I left when the effects of the pipe had worn off. Past experience has taught me it is not a good idea to walk home soon after the pipe. Last time I did that, I followed the frolicking English women into the woods and wound up spending the night in a hollowed out log.

As I neared our camp I saw a bonfire on the hill. Apparently the Christians would not be the only ones worshipping this week. I neared my cabin, and felt something immediately amiss. My door had been knocked down. I ran inside and the place was in disarray. Broken furniture, sword marks in the walls, and fresh blood on the ground. I ran out of the cabin and looked for Otter; he was nowhere in sight. I ran through our makeshift town and grabbed the first person I saw. He was a balding man in his late forties. His build was rather meek; this seemed to match his disposition. I held him by both arms and tried to get him to look me in the eyes. He would not meet my gaze. This man knew something.

"What happened in my cabin?" I said loudly as I began to tighten my grip on his arms.

"What could I do?" He whined, "I'm only one man, nobody else wanted to get involved..."

I began to shake him violently. "What happened?" I said as loud as I could.

"I...I...I can't tell you or I will be next." He winced with pain as I tightened my grip on his arms.

I pushed him against a nearby wall, pulled my dagger and cut him lightly across his face.

"With God as my witness, if you don't tell me what I want to know, you will be dead in the next few moments." I meant every word. I placed my blade under his throat so that he knew it.

"They are sacrificing to odinn," he choked, as the pressure of the blade made speaking difficult, "Your son has been chosen as sacrifice."

I left him there cowering and fearing the retribution from those who worshipped an imagined god. I ran towards the bonfire—I did not believe that I had enough time to call my men. As I got closer, I saw the tree bent down with a figure tied to it. There was a crowd of worshippers between Otter and myself and there was a man in a hat giving invocations to odinn and holding a knife. I wasted no time on thought. I drew my sword, and ran straight at the crowd of worshipers and hacked at the first one I came to. He fell dead, his head split down the middle. At that point, I moved on instinct and training. My sword and I became one. We spun and twirled in a deadly dance. My blade found its mark over and over again. Rik had taught me well. His style of fighting was ideal against multiple foes, and this day I was heavily outnumbered.

I had spun my way through about half the crowd. Most were losing any interest they may have had in stopping my progress toward their intended victim. Those who did oppose me came at me in clumsy charges. A raven haired man ran at me full speed, his sword above his head. I spun to his right and sliced his stomach during my spin. His intestines came spilling out as he fell dead.

I would soon be at the tree. Not soon enough though. Rig recognized that I was not going to stop. He screamed his last prayer to odinn and raised his knife to cut the rope that held the tree. I was not close enough to stop him, and he would have time to run away once my boy was hung.

Just as he had brought the knife up, there was a blood-chilling scream. A figure flew in from the top of the bonfire flames. Terror welled up in Rig's eyes as streaks of feathers, flames and claws came at him. His talons raked Rig's face, leaving him bloody, and knocked the hat from his head.

Rig crumpled to the ground, but still had the knife. I had just dispatched with the last of those stupid enough to oppose me and was running up the hill.

Rig got to his feet. He still had time to cut the rope. He once again raised his blade. I screamed at the top of my lungs for him to stop. He scowled at me, and then just as he was about to drop the sharp blade on the rope, he fell backwards. It was as if he were slapped by an invisible hand.

This confused me for a moment. I stopped my run, fearing some trick. It was dark and it took my eyes a moment to adjust to what I was seeing. I stalked a little closer and could hear him breathing heavily and saw him tugging at something. It wasn't long before I was close enough to see his problem. There was a Skraeling arrow imbedded in his stomach. I looked around for the shooter, but he had disappeared into the forest, as expected.

I walked up to Rig and stepped on the hand with the knife. I removed his weapon. I felt the urge to kick him in the head. I didn't fight it. He rolled over on his side after the kick. Rig was nearly unconscious, but was still writhing and pulling at the arrow in his gut. I walked around him and saw the wound David had left on his face. He had been cut to the bone by David's talons. I also got a better look at the tattoo on his right shoulder. He kept it covered nearly as often as he did his head. The tattoo had always seemed familiar, but I could never place it. Now, with the flames reaching into the sky and the scent of death in the air, my memory of this mark of the raven is stirred. It was back when I was a child. I had followed Rik into town; he led me to the place where Danish sailors had been executed. They hung in the trees, along with their colors. Their flag bore the same raven that now decorated Rig's shoulder. This brought up more than a few questions, but first I tended to Otter.

I left Rig and freed Otter from the rope. I took care not to cut it, it still had a use this night. Otter was beaten and nearly unconscious, but alive. I laid him down and told him we would be home soon.

Grabbing Rig by the feet, I dragged his unconscious form to where Otter had been tied. He started to come to just as I was tying his feet. I rolled him over and began to tie his hands. It was starting to sink in with him just what I was doing. He began to plead and bargain for his life as the rope was tied around his neck. It was then that I got a good look at the back of his bald head.

147

He had three long and deep scars. I turned him around and wiped the blood from his face. Then I tore his shirt open and looked at the scars on his chest. They matched. They were the marks left by David's attacks. This was Rik's killer. David had known all along. Rig's hats were a ruse to keep his scars from anyone's notice. I will bet that Leif knew all along.

David landed upon my shoulder as I grabbed Rig's throat. My only question to him was why did he kill Rik. He pleaded and cried as he answered. He screamed how it wasn't his fault, and that if Rik had continued paying the Danes, nothing would have happened. Rig blamed Rik for double crossing the Danes. Rik would pay them tribute, in return for them not sinking his trading ships. This went on for months. Rik even got to the point of employing the Danes to carry freight for him. Rig looked to the sky as he screamed that Rik was their friend. He continued his telling of the story with the day Rik gave them directions to what was a safe harbor in Greenland. But when they dropped their anchor, warships of Eirik the Red came from nowhere and destroyed them all. In the end, Rig just repeated over and over again that he was doing his duty.

I finished tying the rope around his neck and wasted no more time or words on him as I cut the rope that held the tree to the ground. I watched it launch him in the air, and heard his neck crack as the rope stopped his momentum. I left him hanging there for the birds to eat. David was the first to partake, then came the ravens.

My emotions were mixed as I picked up Otter. My son was alive and my father vindicated. For this I was relieved. Rik was not a criminal, but acted in the interest of our people by befriending the Danes, then duping them and bringing about their destruction. This explains Eirik's debt to Rik for a service he once performed. The gold I received was most likely Rik's payment for his heroic deed. I became angered by the lies Leif had told me. He manipulated me into coming here despite Rik's service to his family.

I carried Otter back to our cabin. Once he is healed, I will send him home to Greenland.

Chapter 21

Harald the Vindicator, as he came to be known, was the man who raised me to manhood. After my near death at the hands of pagan worshipers, he healed my wounds and had a dispatch of soldiers take the boat and me back to Greenland. He sent his journal along with me so that I would not forget him. He also sent a message for Leif Eiriksson. It simply said that he would no longer lead the colonists and he had better get someone over there in quick order. Harald never returned to Greenland. He felt betrayed by Leif for lying and allowing the killer of his adoptive father to not only live, but to serve under him.

Harald developed a rather close bond with the Skraelings and eventually went to live with them. He married the chief's daughter and had many strong children.

I became the captain of my own ship and ran supplies to the dying colony in Vinland. It never again had strong leadership and was therefore doomed.

Warfare with the Skraeling's once again became a constant annoyance, and the colony was disbanded in the year of our lord 1020. After that there were sporadic, unsuccessful settlements, but never a serious colonization effort.

I would visit as often as I could and was there when Harald the Vindicator died as a very old man in the year 1066.